Murder Uncorked

A TOAST to MURDER

MICHELE SCOTT

BERKLEY PRIME CRIME, NEW YORK

THE BERKLEY PUBLISHING GROUP
Published by the Penguin Group
Penguin Group (USA) Inc.
375 Hudson Street, New York, New York 10014, USA
Penguin Group (Canada), 90 Eglinton Avenue East, Suite 700, Toronto, Ontario M4P 2Y3, Canada
(a division of Pearson Penguin Canada Inc.)
Penguin Books Ltd., 80 Strand, London WC2R 0RL, England
Penguin Group Ireland, 25 St. Stephen's Green, Dublin 2, Ireland (a division of Penguin Books Ltd.)
Penguin Group (Australia), 250 Camberwell Road, Camberwell, Victoria 3124, Australia
(a division of Pearson Australia Group Pty. Ltd.)
Penguin Books India Pvt. Ltd., 11 Community Centre, Panchsheel Park, New Delhi—110 017, India
Penguin Group (NZ), 67 Apollo Drive, Rosedale, North Shore 0632, New Zealand
(a division of Pearson New Zealand Ltd.)
Penguin Books (South Africa) (Pty.) Ltd., 24 Sturdee Avenue, Rosebank, Johannesburg 2196,
South Africa

Penguin Books Ltd., Registered Offices: 80 Strand, London WC2R 0RL, England

A TOAST TO MURDER

A Berkley Prime Crime Book / published by arrangement with the author

PRINTING HISTORY
Berkley Prime Crime mass-market edition / April 2010

Copyright © 2010 by Michele Scott.
Wine descriptions copyright © by John Ash.
Cover illustration by Robert Crawford.
Interior text design by Kristin del Rosario.

ISBN: 978-0-425-23392-4

BERKLEY® PRIME CRIME
Berkley Prime Crime Books are published by The Berkley Publishing Group,
a division of Penguin Group (USA) Inc.,
375 Hudson Street, New York, New York 10014.
BERKLEY® PRIME CRIME and the PRIME CRIME logo are trademarks of Penguin Group
(USA) Inc.

PRINTED IN THE UNITED STATES OF AMERICA

10 9 8 7 6 5 4 3 2 1

One

DO *you believe in fate? Sincerely, Moros Apate Thanatos.* Nikki stared at the old photo beneath the note—a newspaper photo of a bride and groom. Her groom— Derek Malveaux smiling at the camera, arm around ex-wife Meredith Malveaux on their wedding day. And the signature. How weird. *Moros Apate Thanatos.* Greek. Had to be Greek. Nikki didn't know what the words meant exactly, but the word *Moros* didn't sound good. She could jump on the computer and look it up. Whatever. It was some weirdo trying to shake her up before her wedding day. Why? Well it *was* sort of a known fact around wine country that Nikki had a knack for playing amateur sleuth and she was pretty decent at it. Maybe someone was testing her skills. But she didn't have time for any type of mystery right now. She had a wedding to plan for goodness sakes.

Nikki shook her head and crumpled up the piece of

paper and photo. She checked the postmark. Nothing. No return address. She frowned as the phone rang. In the background, Oscar the Grouch was singing something about trash. She glanced at her little charges who appeared to be entranced by the show.

If this was another one of those blocked caller calls, she thought she might come undone. For two weeks now, she'd been getting one to two phone calls a day. Of course after receiving what she just had in the mail, she had to wonder if it was Meredith who'd caught wind that in a few days Nikki and Derek were to be wed. But she didn't see how that was possible. Meredith was in prison for murdering Gabriel Asanti, the former winemaker at Malveaux. Not to mention she and her half brother had tried to murder both Nikki and Derek. No. It seemed to Nikki that the only way Meredith and her disturbed brother Cal Winters could be behind the ominous note and prank phone calls was if they had someone on the outside doing their dirty work for them. But what for? The two of them were locked up for life. Maybe she would get on the Internet later and check out the meaning behind the signature on the notes.

Nikki grabbed the phone off the Spanish tiled kitchen counter, checking the caller ID first. She sighed. "Hi, Simon. Violet is fine. I haven't corrupted the poor girl yet, but if you don't stop bothering me, I might," she said. She opened up the garbage disposal and threw away the note and photo.

"You're such a peach. Listen Snow White, I want tails on my tux. As your best man, I mean maid of honor"—he giggled—"I think tails are necessary. They're elegant, royal, regal, and totally appropriate."

"No. No tails." She glanced up to see what the toddlers were doing.

"Oh no! No, no, no, baby!" She dropped the phone and dashed from behind her kitchen counter and into the family room where the little ones were getting into things they shouldn't have been. She had a fleeting vision of her favorite pinkberry lipstick smeared on the cream colored rug.

She took her purse from her friend Alyssa's three-year-old son Petie.

"Petie wants the purse," he whined. "Petie wants your purse, Aunt Nikki."

"No honey. This is Aunt Nikki's purse. It's not a toy."

Then two-year-old Violet stuck out her lower lip, crocodile tears filling her eyes. "Oh, sweetie girl. No tears." Nikki picked her up. Violet Nicole Malveaux was the newest family member to join the vineyard.

Nikki's best pals Simon and Marco had come home from China with Violet a little over a month ago. Simon was not only Nikki's BFF, but was soon to be her maid of honor and her brother-in-law. Both Simon and Marco had wanted badly to be parents. They'd been jumping through the hoops within the U.S. system, but because they were gay they faced even more issues adopting than straight couples did. No one ever spoke out loud about these "issues," but they had become obvious to her dear friends after nearly eight months of getting nowhere. The guys had even asked Nikki to be a surrogate, but there was no way she was down for that. Nikki wanted a child with Derek, and they'd been trying to conceive for some time now. They both felt that the sooner they started trying to have a family, the better. The doctors had told Nikki she would likely have some difficulty getting pregnant.

Two couples wanting to become parents—and Simon and Marco had done just that. Since they didn't think they were ever going to adopt a child from their own country, and since a surrogate looked to be out of the question, they decided that maybe pulling a Brangelina and adopting a child from another country would be the way to go. And it had been. They both fell in love with little Violet at first sight. She was pretty much impossible not to fall in love with, with her big brown eyes, her dark hair that hung in wisps around her sweet face, and her precious laugh that could put a smile on even the most jaded of people. Now Violet was a Malveaux and Nikki would be a Malveaux in a matter of days because this coming Saturday was her wedding day! Tomorrow friends of Derek's would be arriving from out of town and there was so much left to do.

But before she could get back to the wedding plans, she needed to take charge of the toddlers in the house. Why she'd agreed to babysit both Violet and Petie she wasn't sure. Well, yes she was. She loved kids. Petie's mom Alyssa had gone in for the final fitting of her bridesmaid's dress, and Simon headed in with her for his final fitting of his maid of honor tuxedo. Yes, Simon was going to be Nikki's maid of honor, and Marco was to be Derek's best man. A little bit unconventional maybe, but not much went on at the Malveaux vineyard that could be considered conventional or, for that matter, even really functional. But they had a lot of damn fun.

"Nikki, Nikki . . ."

"Oops. Come on gang." She walked back into the

kitchen where she'd dropped the phone, forgetting all about Simon and his tirade over the fact that he wasn't going to be wearing tails.

He was screaming her name into the phone. "Nikki!"

"I'm here." Violet leaned her head against Nikki's shoulder and wrapped her arms around her, entwining her fingers into her hair. The baby had taken to playing with Nikki's hair and many times it helped her fall asleep. Simon stopped by on occasions when he couldn't get her to go down for a nap and asked if she could play with her auntie's hair in order to lull her. They joked about Simon needing to get a long haired wig. "Just a sec, Simon. Petie, sit down at the table okay, and Auntie Nikki will get you a snack. Hold on for one minute."

Petie smiled. "Okay. Petie wants a snack." He batted his lashes over his big brown eyes. Oh, boy, the kid was going to be a heartbreaker.

"I know. Hang on." Nikki picked the phone back up. "Hi. Sorry."

"What in the world is going on there?" Simon sounded like he was hyperventilating.

"Nothing. Petie got into my purse while talking to you and he took my lipstick out and dumped most of my purse onto the floor. No worries. I'll pick up the mess in a minute. I think Violet is falling asleep on me. She's tired from playing all morning. I need to put her down, and Petie is waiting for a snack."

"Why didn't you put your purse away in the first place, Snow White?" he asked, referring to her by his pet name for her. "I mean, seriously. You have babies there and God knows what could be growing in your purse. Or what if one of them took out a pen or pencil and stabbed themselves in the eye? The possibilities are endless. I can't believe you would be so irresponsible."

"I don't have time for one of your lectures on parenting right now. You can scold me later. If you hadn't called with your drama in the first place, I wouldn't be irritated with you and having to pick up the contents of my purse." Nikki knew those contents ranged from umpteen receipts, candy and gum wrappers, a lipstick or two, business cards, and some loose change. She was notorious for dumping anything and everything into what Derek called her "abyss" instead of her purse. Thus, Simon wasn't completely off base with his accusation of things possibly growing in there.

"Speaking of my drama, I want those tails," he demanded.

"No. It's my wedding. I said no, and now I have to go. Bye-bye." She hung up the phone and then turned the ringer off. "Ha-ha. Too bad, so sad." She faced Petie. Violet's fingers were still wound in her hair, but she'd grown quiet and become deadweight against her.

She needed to put her down, but would have to walk into the guest room where her playpen was and Petie had started banging his fists on the kitchen table. "Snack. Petie wants snack. Petie wants snack."

"Shh, Petie. Violet is going night night. I'm getting you a snack." Balancing the toddler in her arms, she went to the kitchen pantry and took out a box of animal crackers, and got him a glass of milk. "I'm going to go put Violet down now."

"No, no. Petie wants Aunt Nikki here. You sit. You sit right here with Petie. Please." He smiled.

How could she refuse? "Okay. I'll sit."

They shared the animal crackers, and when Petie was finished with his milk, they went to the couch where they sat back and fell asleep watching the rest of *Sesame Street*. The show was Petie's favorite and Elmo was Petie's favorite muppet. On the show Elmo always refers to himself in the third person, as in, "Elmo wants," or "Elmo likes." Thus, Petie had become Elmo's copycat.

He was an adorable little boy who'd been through a great deal in his short life. He had a rare heart condition, and for the first couple of years of his life, he needed a transplant. He had finally gotten one last year, and since then he'd grown stronger and precocious, which was good all around.

With Derek in tow, it was Ollie, Nikki and Derek's Rhodesian ridgeback who woke them when he came bounding into the house, the sound of his nails clicking against the hardwood floors. Nikki opened her eyes to see Derek leaning over her, his green eyes warm and happy, his smile bright. "Look at you. You look good like this."

"Like what?" she asked, sleep on the edge of her voice.

He touched Violet's dark head of hair, and she stirred at his touch. "Mommied out. You are in the mommy zone, and I am liking it. Except the mess is kind of . . ." He made a face.

"I know. They dumped out my purse."

"Want me to pick it up?"

"No. I'll get it."

He leaned in and whispered in her ear, "You know what? Seeing you like this makes me wanna practice those baby-making techniques."

"Easy does it there. We have wedding plans to finish

up, and I think we should wait to practice on our wedding night."

"I disagree, but don't have time to argue. Just got a call from my out-of-town friends, my college buddies and their wives." He made another face, likely realizing that his news would not be exactly welcomed. "Sorry, honey, looks like they decided to come in a day early before everyone else gets in. I have to run into the city now to get them at the airport."

"What? No. No. I'm not ready for guests. Not yet. Look at me. I have peanut butter on my jeans and—"

"You're great. You're gorgeous. Absolutely, positively gorgeous. And it'll take me time to get into the city, pick them up, and come back. That should give you plenty of time to change your jeans. Don't worry about a thing. They're staying at the hotel, and I've already talked to Marco. He'll have their suites ready for them by the time they get here. You don't have to do a thing."

"I think I need to do a little more than change my jeans. What about dinner? I need to go to the store. We don't have a thing for me to fix."

He shook his head. "Stop worrying. I've already taken care of that, too. It's all good. This is our week. Relax. This will be the best week of our lives." He bent down, traced her check and jaw with his finger. "I love you. And I still think we should negotiate the baby making practice. I really do. We'll talk. Or other things." He kissed her, melting the worries away for a few seconds until he said good-bye and walked back out the door.

Ollie plopped down at her feet. "Easy for him to say. No worries. I haven't even told him that Simon wants to wear tails." The caramel colored Ridgeback thumped his tail.

"You wouldn't want to wear tails. Seriously, what normal guy wants to wear tails? Oh wait, though. We are speaking of Simon." Ollie lifted his head and turned toward the door.

"I heard that." It was Simon, gallivanting his way through the hall and into the family room where Nikki was beginning to feel a bit weighted down by team toddler. "Normal is passé, and I am hip and hot."

"Tails are passé."

"Never. Not in a million years. Lookie here. How cute. I just passed the blushing groom-to-be. Uh-oh. I see the bride is not blushing. What gives?"

Nikki didn't get a chance to explain about Derek's friends coming into town or the note and photo, because Violet woke up and heard one of her daddies. "Daddy," Violet said. She called Simon "Daddy," and Marco, "Papa."

Simon reached his arms out. "There is my little rosebud. How is Daddy's little girl? Come here, Vivi."

Violet tried to pull her hands from Nikki's hair to go into her father's arms. "Ouch," Nikki said. Violet whimpered. "What in the world? I think her hands are stuck." Nikki looked up at Simon.

"What do you mean?" Simon asked.

"I don't know. But I can't get them loose." Violet kept trying to free her hands but couldn't, and she began to cry. "They're stuck in my hair."

"Was she playing with glue?"

"Of course not."

Simon reached behind Nikki's back. "Lean forward a little."

Nikki did so. "What's the problem?" Now Violet was starting to really cry and Petie was waking up.

"Hmmm."

"What is it?"

"Um, Snow White . . ." He clucked his tongue. "It appears we definitely have a bit of a sticky situation."

Two

SEATED in the beauty shop with clumps of her hair missing, Nikki swallowed hard. This was so not good. The clumps were up high, too. The sticky situation had turned out to be bubble gum from her purse. Petie explained, after he stopped crying from being woken up in not the gentlest of ways, that he had found the gum, chewed it, and had given Violet a few pieces. Thankfully Violet hadn't swallowed and choked on it. Not so thankfully, the gum had made it into Violet's sticky fingers and then into Nikki's hair. The gum had gone unnoticed for over an hour while they slept, giving it plenty of time to cement onto her hair. Simon had to cut Nikki's hair out of Violet's hands, all the while scolding Nikki on how badly it all could have gone. He backed off when Nikki spouted tears. She wasn't notorious for crying, but lately with all the pressure of the wedding and guests flying in, it didn't take much to set her off. And news flash to Simon—having her past the shoulders long hair cut within a few inches of the scalp only a few days before the biggest day of her life is sort of a big deal. Just a tad.

Simon now sat on the sofa in the salon, reading a copy of *Brides* and drinking a latte. Marco had picked up Violet and taken her back to work at the Malveaux Hotel and Spa. He'd been working hard to have all of the rooms ready for the guests that would be arriving over the next few days, including Nikki's Aunt Cara and her new beau who would be arriving some time the following afternoon.

Unable to get in to see her regular hairdresser on such short notice, she couldn't help but feel a bit skeptical as she sat in a different stylist's chair. Blanche was in her fifties and nice enough, but Nikki had noticed the lady who'd left before her—eighty something, hair coiffed into a wavy, perfect silvery head of hair that was perfect for an eighty-year-old. Fingers crossed Blanche also did hair for a younger set.

Nikki couldn't watch as Blanche picked up the scissors and hacked away. She closed her eyes tight.

Forty minutes later, Simon stood over her, fingers on his chin and looking pensive. Nikki stared in the mirror as Blanche grabbed a bottle of hairspray and started to lacquer the new do.

"Very soccer mom, honey," Simon said.

Nikki didn't have the heart to reply. It wasn't even soccer mom chic. Not even close. It reminded her of the Dorothy Hamill cut she'd had when she was ten. The tears welled up again.

"What's a matter, don't you like it?" Blanche asked.

Simon handed her a hundred bucks and grabbed Nikki's hand. "She loves it." They made it to his car. "This isn't going to work." Nikki couldn't comment. "Let me think for a minute. He slammed his hands against the roof of the Porsche. "I've got it!" Simon flipped open his phone and dialed. "Hi. Maximilian, please." A few seconds passed. "Max. It's me, Simon Malveaux, and I have a *huge* problem. Like ginormous." He went on to explain Nikki's hair dilemma. "Uh-huh. I understand." He paused. "I could probably hook you up with some wine for your cellar. The Cab is divine. You are right. Certainly. Will do. You are a lifesaver. We'll see you within the hour."

"Where are we going?" Nikki mustered. "And who did you just promise a case of wine to?"

"Where we should have gone in the first place. I don't know what I was thinking. I wasn't thinking. Brain fart or lack of sleep from the wee one getting up at night." He shook his head.

"Simon!"

"What? Get in the car. We have to hurry. I cannot believe that I allowed you to go to that Podunk of a salon. That's not even a salon. It's barely a step up from a barbershop. Not even in Supercuts' category! Good Lord in heaven. No need to worry, because I am going to take care of this. And it's three cases of wine and well worth it. Trust me."

Another hour and Nikki was at another salon. This one was contemporary in style—all reds, blacks, whites, and lots of chrome and silver. It was a hubbub of activity, and Simon explained that Maximilian Werlin was simply the best that the wine country had to offer.

"Oh, darling, Simon was right. I am so glad he brought you here. Who did this to you? That's hideous. Call me Max." He stuck out his manicured hand and gave her a limp handshake. Max was polished from his head down to his toes with golden waves of hair that skimmed his shoulders. He looked to be wearing mascara around his dark blue eyes. He looked like he'd spent either time in the tanning booth on a regular basis, or used that spray-on tan that gave off an orange glow. He wore dark jeans that appeared to be plastered on, and a tight white tee. A diamond stud glimmered in his left ear. "Now, I don't do hair any longer. I don't need to. I run all of the show here." He waved his arms flamboyantly in the air. He basically scared the hell out of Nikki. "The little people listen to *moi*. I would have loved for you to see Shereen but she's booked, so I'm going to take you over here and have you take a seat at our newest designer's chair."

"Designer? It's my hair not my house."

Max looked at Simon and paused for a second until Simon started laughing and rolling his eyes. Max followed suit. "She's adorable. Where did you find her?"

"She's marrying my brother. This weekend."

"Love it. Lovely. Darling, let's pink you up."

"Pink me up?"

Max laughed again. "Oh, how much fun are we gonna have." He clapped his hands. "Know what? I am not going to take you over to Chi-Chi's chair."

"Chi-Chi?" Nikki thought she was in some type of bad sitcom.

"Yes. Our darling Chi-Chi. Isn't that a great name?"

"For a Lhasa apso."

"Adorable." Max pointed at her and winked at Simon. "Simon grab me that towel and drape it over that mirror. She's all mine." He pointed to a mirror in front of one of the stations. "We're going to have a little fun together, and I get to change your life for the better. Top Model Makeover."

"Goodie. Simon," she growled. "Top Model Makeover?"

"You don't watch Tyra? Come on. When they make over the models? Have you been stuck in a closet?" Max shook his head.

Nikki glared at Simon.

He bent over and whispered in her ear, "It's going to be fine. Trust me. When have I ever led you astray?"

"Do you really want me to answer that?" She sighed. "I have to be back soon. Derek's friends will be arriving."

"Hush. You are a bride to be. Your man can wait and I will make it worth his while. You are now in the hands of a master." Max took a bow. "Allow me to work my magic. Why don't you pour her a glass of wine, Simon? There's a lovely Rosé in the fridge and make sure you grab a slice of the apple galette with some aged Gouda. I have Bouchon do all of my catering, and I make certain that my clientele does not leave here without a perfect do, a little buzz, and a full tummy." He rubbed his stomach. "Life doesn't get any better than that."

"I agree," Simon replied.

Nikki felt nauseous. "I don't need any wine or galette and cheese."

"Nonsense." Max's eyes narrowed. "Get her the wine and the galette."

Simon scurried off.

Nikki sighed. "Can you take the towel off the mirror? I'm a big girl. I can handle this."

"No no." He shook a finger in her face. "When I work with a client—which is so rare because remember I am the boss man now, el jefe—anyway, when I work with a client, this is how I do it. You have to trust that I am going to create art, a masterpiece, and you will be stunned into bliss."

Nikki's stomach clenched. "Whatever." At this point, anything this Max character did to her couldn't be any worse than what Blanche had done, and so she sat down and let Picasso do his thing.

Simon brought her back the wine and galette. "Taste it!" Max ordered. Nikki did and was pleasantly surprised. She smiled and nodded. "I told you, didn't I? And how pretty is that pink in that wine? It's like a hue from a sunset blazing across the sky. Divine, darlings."

An hour and a half later, two glasses of wine and begging for another slice of galette, Simon continuously shook his head and reminded her that the big day was approaching. "You do not want to be getting chubby, my friend."

"Please," she begged.

"Can I have tails?"

"No."

"Then, nooooo back at you."

"Fine."

"Are we ready?" Max asked.

Nikki had been washed, clipped, sprayed, and whatnot, and now it was time for the reveal. She looked to Simon first and he seemed to be coming out of his skin.

"I love it, I love it. It feels so vavavavoom, doesn't it? Sexy. It is *hot,* baby, *hot!*"

Max smiled smugly. "I told you." He grabbed the towel over the mirror and yanked back. "Voila!"

Nikki's mouth fell open. She stared for a few seconds and brought her fingers to her hair. "That's not me," she said. "My hair. Me? What?" Two glasses of wine shouldn't make her see things.

"Looks like we can't call you Snow White anymore. Not even Goldilocks." Goldilocks had been his original nickname for Nikki when she'd arrived at the vineyard with golden blond hair a few years ago, before going back to her original dark hair.

Nikki just sat there staring, shocked.

"You can call her Gwen or Pink or Blondie," Max said. "Look at her. Does she not look like a rock star?"

"Or a porn star," she said, breaking her silence. "I don't want to look like a rock star. I want to look like me."

Max took a step back. "Porn star! Please. Ridiculous."

Nikki shook her head—her newly platinum blond, pixie-short-hair head. "Okay, I can get with the haircut. Fine. It's not soccer mom." It was sort of cute, and she had secretly always wanted a short do, but figured she'd wait until after the wedding. Derek loved her long hair. Oh no. Derek. What was he going to say? "But platinum? Couldn't we do my normal color?"

"Honey, your big day is around the corner and you need to make a splash. The camera is going to love you."

She sighed. "Right. But can we darken this up? A bit?"

Max frowned and put his hands on his hips. "No, we can't." He glanced over at Simon. "Suddenly not so adorable, and suddenly I am out of time and patience. You look like a rock star and that'll be two hundred and fifty dollars. And by the way, I wouldn't try to color over that any time soon. Your hair could fall out or turn green. Simon, you can drop my wine off here at the *salon*."

Nikki wrote him a check and stormed out with Simon following her. "Look at me. Rock star, porn star, whatever star. Not the image I wanted for my wedding day. And two hundred and fifty bucks, plus three cases of wine! I don't think so. He gets no wine." She shook a finger at him. "Not a drop!"

"You look amazing. You do. You'll get used to it. I'll take you to go see my friend Tanya and she'll give you some new makeup tips to go with the hair."

"I'm done with *your* people."

"Should have put the purse away then, bridezilla."

"No kidding, brainiac."

They drove the rest of the way home in silence. Nikki got out of the car and headed into the house where she could hear laughter inside. Great. Just great. Derek had made it back with his friends. She turned to run back to Simon's Porsche, but he peeled out and drove away. Maybe she had been a little ungrateful. A little bit selfish and it *had* all been her fault, but it was her hair and now her hair was really blond and really short and . . . This was not good.

She walked around back and went into the house through the side door. She made it to their bedroom bathroom without being noticed, where she played around for a minute with her hair and tried to get past the shock of seeing herself like this. She put on some makeup and changed into a tea-length, black spaghetti strapped dress she planned to wear out for the evening. Their dinner reservations were in an hour, but first she had to let Derek know about her hair before she walked out into the family room and he didn't recognize her. She took out her cell phone and dialed the house phone. The rings echoed. She should've called him before getting home, but she'd been too scared. He'd loved her long hair. He twirled it around his fingers at night, and she loved having him play with it. Now it was gone. Oh, for goodness sakes, it was only hair. She frowned, but it was *her* hair and now she had pixie short, blond hair only a few days before *her* wedding.

"Honey, where are you? I've been calling your cell and I was starting to get worried. My friends are here and they're dying to meet you."

"I have to tell you something," she said, sitting down on the end of their bed.

"What is it? Are you okay?"

"I don't know."

"Where are you?" he asked.

"In the bedroom."

"The bedroom?"

"Yes. Our room. Please don't let anyone know I'm in here."

"Nikki?" She heard him walking down the hall and come into their room. "Nikki?" She looked up at him. "Wow, your hair," he said sounding stunned. He hung up the phone and stood looking at her. She wasn't sure what the look on his face meant. Did he hate it? Was he angry? Amused? She didn't know.

"I know." She started to tear up again. "Violet had gum in her hands and she put them in my hair and, oh, God. It's a long story, but this is the result." She tossed up her hands.

Derek came over to her and cupped his hand under her chin. She looked up at him. Vulnerability wasn't something she typically resorted to, but at that moment she couldn't help feeling childlike and weak. She kept trying to remind herself that it was only hair. "You look beautiful. Bald, blond, short, long, blue, green, I don't care. I love it. I love you."

"But you loved my long hair."

He nodded and sat down next to her. "Like I said, it's you not your hair that I am marrying, and honestly I think you look great. Sexy. It's *really* sexy." He planted a kiss on her. Everyday Derek showed her more and more why she'd chosen to marry him. "Come on, let's go. I want you to meet my friends. You're going to love them and they're going to love you, Pink."

"Pink?"

"The pop star. Your hair." He winked.

"Now I get it. Simon," she growled.

"Simon?"

"Yes. Your brother was the one who told the hair-dresser to Pink me up. At the time I had no clue what he meant. If I'd known . . ."

"I should have known my brother had something to do with this."

"You hate it, don't you?"

"I told you that I think it's great. When did you get all

insecure on me? Now come on, beautiful." He took her hand and led her out into the family room.

"Everyone this is my gorgeous soon-to-be wife, Nikki," Derek said as they walked into the open family room where two couples were seated on their distressed leather sofas, a photo album in one of the women's laps. Ollie their dog was not necessarily one for company and he was off sulking in the kitchen. Being on the sofa was a right he felt was his alone, and sharing it, particularly with strangers, was an affront as far as he was concerned. When he saw Nikki, he walked in from the kitchen and started to growl.

"It's me, bud. It's me." Ollie then wagged his tail and sauntered over to her where he sat down next to her and licked her hand.

"Nikki just had her hair done and the silly ridgeback here doesn't recognize her."

The woman on the couch with the photo album, set it aside and stood, stretching out her hand. "I'm Savannah," she said with a Southern accent. Savannah was petite, sort of delicate except for her large boobs. She had ivory skin, long strawberry blond hair curled around her shoulders, big blue eyes, and an expertly made-up face. She wore a two-piece knit ensemble in lavender, reminding Nikki of an Easter egg. "You certainly don't look like your pictures." She smiled a tight-lipped smile.

Oh, great. This was someone Nikki was going to actually have to spend an entire evening with. She nodded. "I know. Mishap."

Savannah frowned. "Hmmm. Poor dear."

"I love it." Derek smoothed his hand on the back of her head. "Sleek."

"I think she's even more beautiful than her picture." The man seated next to Savannah stood up. "Hi, I'm Tristan. You met my wife here." He put his arm around Savannah's shoulder and pulled her in close.

Tristan didn't exactly fit with the delicate Savannah. He was ruggedly handsome with a three-day-old beard, hazel eyes, dark wavy hair, and he wore a pair of jeans with a navy blue T-shirt. Savannah made a face when he hugged her.

Derek smiled wide. "Tristan and I were known to get into a little trouble back in the day."

"I'll say." Savannah smiled. "Look here. I brought some old photos and an annual from when we were in college." She picked up the album, practically shoved it into Nikki's hands, and pointed at a photo with a bunch of people in it drinking beer.

As Nikki took a closer look, she saw Derek doing a beer bong with college kids all around him laughing, and a pretty dark-haired woman had her hands on his shoulders standing behind him. "Looks like you had a lot of fun." Savannah was next to the woman standing behind Derek in the chair. She was all made up with her boobs practically falling out of her tight tank top. Not exactly the demure woman standing before her now. "Was this your girlfriend?" Nikki asked, pointing to the dark-haired girl.

Derek looked over her shoulder. "No. That's Nancy. She was going out with our friend Zach. In fact, they got married. I invited them to the wedding, too. It looks like only Nancy is attending though. I don't know where she's staying because they live in L.A. I doubt she's driving up and then heading back. That's a long drive."

"Divorce," Savannah said. "I still talk with Nance and it's kind of an ugly deal." She waved her hand in the air. "She just filed. I think she told me she's staying up at Calistoga Ranch."

"Why didn't she just make reservations here?" Derek asked.

"Maybe she wants some alone time. Like I said, it's been a bit of a rough year." Savannah flipped her hand in a nonchalant manner.

"Don't you think it's weird that she's coming and not Zach?" Tristan said. "I mean he was our friend. She was just the girlfriend and subsequently the wife who now isn't the wife."

"Oh my God, Tristan, you can be so ridiculous sometimes. Nancy was friends with Derek, just like both Lily and I were. So are you saying that if we ever got a divorce that I couldn't come to any of these occasions? What if this isn't Derek's last hoorah?"

"It is his last hoorah," Nikki replied impulsively.

"I'm sorry, I didn't mean . . ." Savannah started.

Nikki held up her hand. "No worries. Really. I know you meant nothing by it."

"Enough talk of Zach and Nancy. I don't care which one of them comes. I wasn't close with either of them back in the day. He was always a little too studious for me and she was way too serious," the other man on the couch said. He stood, too, and reached out his hand. "Hi Nikki. I'm Jackson, this is my wife, Lily. Sorry for our walk down memory lane."

Lily also shook Nikki's hand. "Pleasure to meet you."

"Finally a gal who can settle this guy down," Jackson

said. He smiled warmly. He was rounder than Derek or Tristan but pleasant looking. He wore glasses over his brown eyes, had thinning light brown hair, and looked to be a guy who spent a lot of time behind a desk—not much sun on the face. His wife was attractive—golden blond hair, hazel eyes, taller than her husband, her hair pulled back off her face. She looked far more pleasant than Savannah. Although Savannah exuded wealth and snobbery, Lily appeared a bit trendier, wearing a low-cut red dress and strappy sandals. If Nikki didn't know better, she would have thought that Tristan went with Lily and Savannah was married to Jackson. So much for stereotypes.

Nikki put on her Miss Congeniality smile, knowing the guys were important to Derek. The three of them had been fraternity brothers back in college. He'd been really excited about them coming out for the wedding.

"It isn't like this is his first marriage," Savannah said.

Tristan eyed her. "I don't think Meredith counts."

Derek glanced at Nikki.

"Weren't you the one who helped put her behind bars?" Savannah asked directing her question at Nikki.

"Savannah, I don't think either Nikki or Derek wants to talk about that. This is their wedding, their time. Come on. That was such bad business."

"Of course. My apologies."

Nikki tried to maintain her smile while Savannah asked about Meredith, but she couldn't help not only being put off, but also a little shaken as she remembered the note and photo from earlier that day. Maybe she shouldn't have tossed it. She really didn't want to put any type of credibility into it. She'd dig in the disposal when they got back from dinner and get it out.

"Where's Kenny?" Jackson asked. "He e-mailed me and said he was going to go ahead and come on in today, too."

"He is, but not for another couple of hours. Besides, do we really want to take Kenny to dinner with our wives?" Derek asked.

"There're only two wives here," Savannah said coyly and winked at Nikki.

What was it with the Southern belle and her nastiness toward Nikki? Ooh, if Nikki wasn't such a "nice" girl, she'd have bitch slapped her. The thought alone made her smile. "Soon enough though." She cuddled in closer to Derek and decided to strike back a bit. "And I can't wait to be Mrs. Malveaux."

Was Savannah glaring at her?

"Kenny is coming here *tonight*?" Lily asked.

Jackson looked at her. "Of course. We can't have a shindig this size and not have Mr. Party Animal himself."

The guys laughed.

"I think he's obnoxious," Lily said. "I can't stand that guy. I don't know how you all have remained friends with him. He's a total loser."

"Come on, Lil. He's just Kenny and that's why we love him," her husband said.

"Jackson is right. He isn't that bad. A bit off the wall, but I find his behavior charming," Savannah said, butting in.

"Charming?" Lily shook her head. "You've lost your mind, Savannah."

"I think we better get a move on. By the time we get to the restaurant . . ." Derek said.

Savannah turned to Tristan. "Darling, I am not feeling well. I feel a migraine coming on. I think I want to go lie down in the room, maybe get a massage at the spa. It's not too late is it?" she asked Derek.

"No. It isn't, but I'm sorry you don't feel well. I'm sure you can get an appointment. It closes at eight."

She clasped her hands together, her enormous diamond ring sparkling. "Excellent."

"Savvy. Come on, baby. We haven't seen Derek in a few years. Take some aspirin. Come to dinner. Let's get to know Nikki."

She sighed. "Have you ever had a migraine? I don't think so. As lovely as I know dinner will be, I think it's best if I rest, and then I'll be more than happy to get to know Nikki tomorrow. We do have—what is it? Three days here?"

Three days too many. Nikki was pleased the woman was suffering a headache. If she came to dinner, Nikki was afraid she'd be the one needing Tylenol. She decided to put in her two cents. "I do know what migraines are like. We'd love to have you join us, but by all means rest and, yes, we will have plenty of time to spend together." Not if she could help it, they wouldn't.

"Thank you."

"I can stay with you," Tristan said.

"No. I'm fine. Go. Just go." She waved a hand at him, and took the photo album from Nikki, setting it back down on the coffee table. "We can look at this tomorrow. There's some fun stuff in here."

Oh, goody.

They all piled in to Derek's Range Rover and on their way out dropped Savannah at the Malveaux Hotel and Spa, also located on the winery's property.

The property was acres and acres of rolling vineyard. On the highest peak, with a fantastic view of the valley, sat the hotel and spa, done in an old-world Tuscan style that was intended to make guests feel as if they'd really stepped out of the hustle of life and into luxury and relaxation. Farther back from the hotel was the winery where wine tastings were held daily. Connected to the winery were the offices where Nikki and Derek worked. Back behind the offices stood the warehouse and large metal wine vats. And about half a mile from there stood the old mansion where Derek had grown up and which now served as home to Simon, Marco, and Violet. Derek and Nikki's home was a smaller ranch style that was located just behind the front gates and to the side of the entrance of the property, set against a lovely pond that a handful of ducks had made their home.

"The place looks lovely as always," Savannah commented as they took the short drive to the hotel. "I love the addition of the hotel and spa. It's truly exquisite."

"Thank you," Derek replied. "Nikki worked with the decorator and helped design everything."

"Oh yes. I do think that the colors inside could be a bit brighter. They're a tad muted for my taste."

Savannah was definitely scoring points.

"Here we are," Nikki said, ready to place a foot in the back of the woman and kick her out of the car.

"Have a wonderful time," Savannah said.

As she shut the door behind her, Tristan muttered loud enough for everyone to hear, "If you two want to stay in love, whatever you do, don't get married."

Peach Galette with Gouda Cheese
and Bonterra Rosé

What's a bride-to-be to do when she's likely being stalked, her hair is not her own—well it is, but it doesn't look like her own—her fiancé's friends are freaks, and her maid of honor keeps insisting on tails for his tuxedo? Pour herself a good glass of Rosé and slice herself off a piece of peach galette and Gouda cheese. It's decadent, it's divine and, no, it is not low calorie. But what the hell? She's getting married after all.

Whether or not you're a bride-to-be, life has all sorts of stresses. Take some time to be decadent, treat yourself. Like Nikki, you deserve it.

In making their Rosé, Bonterra used a market basket of varietals to contribute surprising complexity to this beautiful salmon-colored wine, focusing in particular on Sangiovese, Zinfandel and Syrah from the Indian Creek vineyard in the Sierra Foothills of Amador County, where they source Syrah as a blender for many of their wines. The knock-your-socks off color is just the beginning. Chilled a bit, the wine reveals aromas and flavors of strawberry, tart cherry, fragrant tea, luscious raspberries, some watermelon, a touch of spice and vanilla in a lingering, unexpectedly joyful finish. Bonterra is serious about making a serious Rosé, and it is time to spread the word that real wine lovers drink Pink. This recipe and pairing would also make a wonderful treat to eat for a bridal shower.

Peach Galette

2 cups unbleached flour
¾ tsp salt
½ cup (1 stick) cold, unsalted butter, cut into small pieces
7 tbsp cold solid vegetable shortening, cut into small pieces
¼ cup ice water
1½ lbs peaches
3 tbsp granulated sugar
1 egg yolk whisked with 1 tsp of water
1 tbsp coarse sugar
¾ lb aged Gouda or Gruyère

To make the dough: In a food processor, combine the flour and salt. Pulse three or four times to blend. Add the butter and pulse a few times, just until evenly distributed and coated with flour. Add the shortening and pulse a few times, until coated with flour. Transfer mixture to a bowl. Drizzle with the ice water while tossing with a fork, just until dough begins to come together in clumps, then knead dough to get it to hold together. Shape into thick round patty, then wrap in plastic wrap and refrigerate for at least two hours.

Preheat oven to 425 degrees. Peel and slice peaches. Set aside.

Put dough on a lightly floured work surface, top with a fresh sheet of plastic wrap, and let stand for ten minutes to warm slightly. Roll dough into a 15-inch circle. Transfer dough to rimless baking sheet. Trim edges as needed to make 15-inch circle, reserving the trimmings. About two inches from the edge of the dough, arrange the peach slices in a neat ring, overlapping the slices slightly. Fill in center with peaches. Sprinkle with granulated sugar.

Gently fold the edge of the dough over the peaches to make a wide border. Make sure there aren't any cracks. Use trimmed dough if needed to patch.

Brush the border with a little egg wash, then sprinkle with coarse sugar. Bake until crust is golden, about 50 minutes. Cool slightly. Serve warm with cheese and wine.

Three

THE five of them had dinner at a new restaurant in St. Helena called Corked. It was upscale, gourmet, painted in creams, sages and golds, with dark hardwood floors and soft lighting. In the bar, a pianist played mellow jazz that carried into the dining area. Almost as soon as Tristan had said the harsh words about marriage, he'd retracted them, and thankfully Jackson's wife Lily was on the ball. She immediately started talking about their home life in upstate New York and their three children, two dogs, and a cat. Lily was normal, cool, sweet, and she and Nikki chatted quite a bit over dinner, as they were seated next to each other. The guys were busy carrying on about the good old days, the fraternity parties and pranks. After some time their stories only amused themselves, and Nikki found herself in conversation with Lily over a glass of Cabernet Sauvignon and a scrumptious grilled pork loin in a sun-dried cherry Cabernet sauce.

"Our kids are great. Ryan is twelve and Katie is ten. Our oldest Jonathan is eighteen, which I can't even believe. We waited a bit after Jon was born to have more children. I wavered at first because I did want to continue the career path. They're all so much fun. Definitely worth it. Ryan is really into hockey and Katie is all about ballet. And Jon is heading off to school in the fall. He's going to Stanford! We are so proud of him. He wants to be an attorney. His dad is bursting with pride. I mean we both are." Lily sipped her wine.

"That's wonderful. Are you a stay-at-home mom?" Nikki asked.

"I am. Yes. Jackson and I decided when I got pregnant with Ryan that it was time for me to lay off the career and stay home. Jon was six by then. I'd been pursuing my career while raising him, but it had kind of exhausted me, trying to balance it all. We knew at that point that we wanted more kids, and we're both from traditional families, so it was a mutual decision."

"What did you do before?" Nikki asked.

"Actually I ran a gym. I was really into bodybuilding, believe it or not, and I had inherited some money from my father's estate, so I opened up a gym. I still work out, but chubby over there has kind of fallen off the wagon. He used to be right in there with me working out daily." She lowered her voice, obviously not wanting to embarrass her husband. "I'm thinking about getting back into it soon now that all of the kids are getting older, and with Jon going off to college, life around the house will probably get a little easier. I work out three days a week with a personal trainer." She made a muscle. "Feel my guns."

Nikki did so, a little embarrassed. The men caught on. "My wife at it again? She loves to let everyone know that she could totally kick my ass if she had to," Jackson said with a laugh. "Did she also tell you that she's a black belt?"

"Really?" Nikki said. "That's something. Impressive."

"I haven't kept on it though. Like I said—kids. And husband and a home, all of that has sort of taken precedence."

Jackson smiled at her and shook his head. "Maybe. But you and I both know you're sneaking those exercise videos when you get a chance. I was thinking of trying one of them myself."

"No need for that, honey. Just get back on that treadmill, especially after eating all that red meat I just saw you consume."

He waved a hand at her and then picked up his wine. "I'm balancing it with red wine."

Everyone laughed and seemed to be having a good time. Tristan had gone a bit quiet, possibly embarrassed by his wife's behavior and his small outburst in the car. When Nikki had a chance, she planned to ask Lily how well she knew Savannah.

The guys went back to their stories and Lily turned to Nikki. "I assume you and Derek want kids. Are you planning on starting a family?"

Ah, the touchy subject. "We've actually been trying."

"Oh." Lily looked surprised. "It's not that I'm super old-fashioned or anything. I mean, actually I was pregnant with Jonathon before Jackson and I got married, but . . ."

Nikki nodded. "I know, kind of the backward way of doing things, even in this day and age. There are some complications. Some medical stuff." She shrugged, not wanting to get into it. The facts were, Nikki had no idea if she would ever get pregnant. They'd been trying for over a year now with no success. They had recently seen a fertility specialist and the plan was for Nikki to begin treatments in hopes of raising her chances of getting pregnant. She and Derek had also discussed adoption after falling as madly in love as they had with Simon and Marco's little Violet.

"I see." Lily grew quiet. "It'll happen. It will. I'm sorry it's so hard. I have never had that problem so I don't know what to say or how it feels." She looked down at her hands in her lap.

Nikki noticed she was wringing her napkin tightly. "It's okay. Thank you, though. It will all work out." She lowered her voice and wanted to change the subject. "How long have you known Savannah?"

"Since college days. Tough one to take. Always has been. Kind of interesting that we both married our college sweethearts. So did our friend Nancy. I'm sorry about Savannah. She was kind of rude to you back at your home. She can be a little difficult." Lily looked up and Nikki followed her gaze. Tristan was looking at them. "We love her though."

Nikki wasn't buying that at all, but figured that Lily didn't want to talk trash about Tristan's wife with him there at the table, although he probably would've joined in. There didn't seem to be any love lost between husband and wife. Nikki hadn't bought her migraine excuse one bit. For one thing, with a migraine coming on, the last thing Nikki knew she would ever want was a massage. When it came to migraines, darkness, no noise, and definitely no one touching her skin.

Nikki took a bite of her pork loin and a decent size sip of Cabernet from her glass. When she looked up, she spotted a handsome, dark-haired man, light eyes, tall, strong looking and full of purpose. He was headed directly to their table. Before she could say anything, Derek saw him, too. He stood up as he said, "Zach? No way, man. What's this?" He spread his arms wide.

Zach smiled wide. He shrugged. "I wouldn't miss the wedding of the century for anything."

Tristan and Jackson stood and shook his hand. "We thought Nancy was coming and because of, you know, the divorce and all, that you bailed out," Tristan said. "Savannah even said that Nancy was staying up in Calistoga. What gives?"

"Jeez, man. Thanks for the warm welcome," he replied. "What gives is that Nancy and I talked. Civilly. And it turns out that she was only coming to get under my skin. I had given in to her because I was tired of fighting over every little piddly thing. She called me up yesterday and told me that I needed to be the one to go. All she was looking for was a vacation, and she decided to take advantage of a time-share we have in Puerto Vallarta. Said she'd rather do that, and that I should fly up here and go to the wedding."

"Glad you did. Good," Derek said. "Good to see you and good to hear that maybe things won't be so hard from here on out."

Zach nodded. "Hope so." He laughed. "I was going to bring this woman I've started seeing, but I knew that would get back to Nancy and she'd come unglued. We just found some smooth waters. I don't want to be rocking that boat."

"Right. Well have a seat. Have some dinner with us. How did you find us?" Derek asked.

"Marco I think his name was. Italian guy at the front desk. Told him who I was and he hooked me up."

"Yeah. Marco is a great guy. He's my brother's partner. You all remember Simon. He was like sixteen I think when I left for college."

"How could we forget?" Jackson said. "Never forget when you had him visit and he fully hit on Kenny."

They all laughed. "Yeah, my brother has never been shy."

"He's settled down a lot," Nikki cut in. She didn't think they were putting Simon down, and even though she was still pretty upset with him over the hair fiasco, she felt a need to come to his defense. "He's got Marco and they just adopted a little girl. Violet."

"That's great. Nancy and I talked about adopting at one point, but she's pretty much on the career track. She works in advertising," Zach said.

Nikki wondered if the couple hadn't been able to get pregnant and that's why they'd considered adoption. Maybe it had caused their problems. That was a thought she didn't want to think. She and Derek had discussed every possibility, and she felt rock solid that no matter what—children or childless—they would love and support one another.

Dinner wound up lasting longer than they'd all planned,

but the food was delicious and the company sans Savannah was delightful. Without his wife, Tristan laughed and talked a lot about his two children as well. Lily and Jackson were fun and good-natured. Lily did come off a little bit pompous, what with the workout stuff, and then she carried on a bit about how she was a room mother for both of her younger kids' classrooms and how she was reportedly the best most organized room parent ever. It did get a little hard to swallow after a while of having to listen to it, but three glasses of wine helped and at least she wasn't rude like Tristan's wife. Zach was interesting and although he'd occasionally refer to his soon-to-be ex-wife, which sort of seemed to weigh him down, he kept things light and lively.

Nikki did think about Derek's friends on the drive back. In reality, they didn't have a lot of people they hung out with in Napa. Either it was just the two of them, or they hung out with Simon and Marco, which Derek had been growing tired of. He could only take so much of his brother. The only other couple they enjoyed being around was Alyssa and her boyfriend, Detective Jonah Robinson.

Most of Derek's friends were more like acquaintances and business associates. Nikki had pretty much lost her best friend Isabel Fernandez when she broke up with Isabel's brother Andrés over a year ago. Nikki had invited her to the wedding, had even called and wanted her to be in the wedding, but Isabel had not returned her call, nor the response card. Nikki was saddened and hurt but understood Isabel's loyalties. She figured it was really unlikely her old friend would show up for her big day.

Nikki wondered what types of friendships they would

cement as a couple over the years. She hoped they could both agree on mutual friends.

Nikki and Derek decided to have nightcap at the hotel wine bar outside by the saltwater pool with Jackson and Lily. Tristan figured that he'd better go and check on Savannah. Zach had gone back to his hotel.

"No problem. Let's all meet for breakfast here around nine, and then Nikki and I can take everyone on a tour of the grounds," Derek said. "I'll call Zach and let him know, too. There'll be room here for him tomorrow to come and stay."

Nikki bit her tongue. She didn't want to remind Derek that she still had a gazillion things to do for the wedding and not much time to do it in. But he'd been so awesome about her hair . . . Oh well, she could humor him and his friends for a couple of hours in the morning.

"Think Kenny has checked in yet?" Jackson asked.

"I don't know. I can check," Derek replied.

They turned the corner, passing a trellis of evening jasmine and a waterfall that spilled down from a group of natural rocks and passed into a stream that recycled through and dumped into the pool. Candle-lit sconces on the golden walls illuminated the way to the pool and bar.

"No. No Kenny. I'm not ready for that. I'm just not," Lily said.

"Who isn't ready for Kenny?" A man in low-riding swim trunks, with a barrel chest, and some hefty arms, looking like a Greek god, walked toward them dripping wet. He had a drink in his hand. "Hey lookie who is here. Jacko baby and the lovely missus." He winked at Lily. She cringed. "And you . . ." He took Nikki's hand. "You must be Miss Nikki Sands." He looked at Derek. "She is hot, man. Totally hot. You lucky SOB. How do you do it? Just make sure this one doesn't try to kill you, too." He winked at her. "If you take him out, though, I'll gladly step in."

"Shut the hell up, Ken." Derek pumped his hand. "I'd hug you, but damn it, go towel off."

"No way. Come here." Kenny wrapped his arms around Derek. "Dude, she is super hot."

Now Nikki cringed and understood completely why Lily found him distasteful. Ironically though, Savannah hadn't. She'd found him *charming*. Even more ironically, she came slinking around the corner and headed to the bar, wineglass in hand and wearing a bikini. So much for the migraine. "You're feeling better?" Nikki asked.

Savannah's eyes widened. "I am, thank you. I guess I was a bit tired is all. I took a nap and then decided to take a dip in the pool because by the time I got up the spa was closed. And look who I found in the pool?" Savannah smiled at Kenny.

"Yeah, man, where's Tristan? What's he thinking leaving his wife here alone?" Kenny said, laughing.

Derek shook his head and eyed Jackson. Nikki watched this exchange with interest. Were men really that stupid? Especially *her* man? Come on. It was so obvious to her. She glanced over at Lily and wondered if she was thinking the same thing.

"Tristan went to check on you," Derek said.

"Here I am." Savannah spread her arms wide.

What had happened to the demure Savannah in all her lavender and perfect makeup? This woman was a completely different specimen. Bikini clad (and not much to the bikini) and no shame waltzing around in it, and her husband nowhere in sight. As far as Nikki was concerned, Derek's friends were a strange bunch. She couldn't wait until tomorrow when her Aunt Cara showed up. Cara might be quirky, but certainly not bizarre.

"Anyone care to join us in the pool?" Savannah asked.

"I would," Jackson replied. "I'm gonna change and grab a beer.

Lily grabbed him by the arm. "No. I don't think so. I think it would be best if we get to bed. It's a big day tomorrow for Nikki and Derek, and they said they wanted to get an early start and show us around the winery and vineyard. We don't need a nightcap anyway."

"Oh, Lil, don't be such a buzzkill," Kenny cut in.

Lily glared at him and then hooked her arm through Jackson's. "Besides, how often do we get to be alone and away from the kids?" She looked at him lovingly.

He smiled. "Good point. Sorry gang. Rain check on the pool."

Kenny shrugged. "Okay, I get that. How about you two lovebirds?" He turned his attention to Nikki and Derek.

Derek put his arm around her. "Nah. I think we better be getting our rest, too."

Tristan showed up right about then. He frowned when he saw his wife without much clothing on, wineglass refilled. "Hey, Kenny! See you found my wife."

Savannah put her free hand on her hip. "It was so funny. I didn't even realize it was him swimming in the pool. I just came down for a hot tub, and after a few minutes he climbed in with me and I realized who it was."

"Your headache over then, I guess?"

Savannah nodded.

"I think we should all get some rest," Tristan said. "I'd hate for your migraine to return."

Savannah frowned.

"Man, you guys are all buzzkills. Back in the day we'd all be up, in the pool, hanging out, having beers until what? Three in the morning." Kenny took a swig of his beer.

"That was almost twenty years ago, my friend. Things change," Derek said.

"They don't have to change that much. You can still have fun."

"I agree with Ken," Savannah said. "Live a little."

"I hate to say it, but here's the deal, we actually have a no-swimming rule here at the hotel after eleven, and it's already eleven thirty. Plus the bar is closing, so I'm going to agree that it's time to get to bed," Derek said.

Nikki sensed that Derek realized Kenny had not only made Lily feel uncomfortable, but that both she and Tristan were not exactly feeling warm and fuzzy toward the "dude" either.

"Don't you own the place? Can't you change the rules when you want? I mean, come on guy, this is your week, your wedding week." Kenny laughed. "Hook a brother up."

"It's my wedding week, too." Nikki was getting tired real fast of this guy's adolescent antics and Savannah's need to play sorority girl. "The thing is we also have a handful of guests at the hotel tonight who are not here for the wedding, so I'm sure you'll understand why we have to follow the policies for tonight at least. Tomorrow night everyone staying here will be wedding guests, so we might be able to fudge things a bit."

"The bride seems a little tense, bro."

Savannah giggled. Nikki shot them both dirty looks. She was over it.

Derek shook his head. "I don't think so. I'm going to be staying here tomorrow night, and I need some sleep for the big day."

"You're staying here tomorrow?" Nikki asked, surprised.

"Of course. Isn't it bad luck to see, I mean sleep, with the bride the night before the wedding?"

"Not even. Sounds like a good plan to me." Kenny pitched in his two cents.

Nikki frowned. She did not like the idea of Derek staying at the hotel with these clowns, especially bad news Kenny. Hmmm.

"We're trying to be a little traditional," Derek said.

"All right. Party tomorrow night, then. I'll be a good boy and go to bed now. You all sleep tight," Kenny said. He made sure he gave Savannah a hug good night, but as he turned back to Nikki and started to try to hug her, she beat him to the punch and stretched out her hand. He looked surprised but she didn't care. Derek's buddy or not, the guy was an ass, and she didn't trust him at all. "The guy is a jerk," Nikki said as soon as they were back to their house.

"He's harmless, honey. He really is." Derek was unbuttoning his shirt.

Nikki already undressed, had pulled on a pair of boxers and one of Derek's T-shirts. She sighed heavily.

"What is it?" he asked.

She wasn't sure how to put this. She really didn't want to start an argument with him, especially since their wedding was just around the corner. The few days leading up to the big day were supposed to be a special time as well, and so far with the hair fiasco, and now the Club Med group's arrival, she wasn't exactly having the most special of times.

"Come on, Nik, what is it? I can tell you're bugged."

She tossed her arms up. "Okay, fine. It's your friends. I'm sorry but I'm not terribly impressed or crazy about some of them. Jackson is a cool guy and his wife is nice, and Zach seems to be okay, but the rest of them are just, I don't know, not my kind of people, I guess."

Now Derek sighed. "By the rest of them, I think you mean Savannah and Kenny. Tristan is not a bad guy. I think he's unhappy, but that doesn't give you a reason to not like the man. As far as Savannah and Kenny, well, people do change some over the years, and I can see where you're coming from. But these are people that I've known for twenty years. I can't just stop being friends with them."

"Why? Like you said, people do change, and maybe it's good to move on and find new friends."

"Here's the thing, Nik. It's not like these people are in our lives or will be on a daily basis. Tristan and Savannah live in Atlanta, Jackson and Lily in New York, and Ken is down in San Diego. Zach is in L.A. But I've had some good times with all of them, and it's my day, too, on Saturday, and I want them there. I want them to see how beautiful you are. I want them to see how happy you make me. I want them to see that I am the luckiest man in the world."

She rolled her eyes at him. "Boy do you have a way with words."

He walked toward her. "I've got a way with other things, too."

"Really now?" Nikki smiled.

"Really."

"Tell me."

"How about I show you?" He winked.

"I guess that'll work."

An hour after Derek showed her his other talents, he snored lightly and Nikki tried to fall asleep. She kept thinking about the next two days and all she had to do. She also kept thinking about Derek's friends and how different they were from him. A bad feeling came over her and sat in her stomach. She tried to think about good things, the actual wedding, the reception, but the feeling wouldn't go away. She had to ask herself, what it was all about? Was it just the things that had gone awry already? Was she worried more unplanned events would occur? Definitely. Or was this what it felt like to get cold feet?

Grilled Pork in a Sun-dried Cherry Cabernet Sauce

Paired with Bonterra Cabernet Sauvignon

Nothing goes better with a flatiron steak than a glass of Cabernet Sauvignon. And when life takes a strange turn, as Nikki's seems to, go ahead and bite off more than you can chew, and definitely pour yourself a great glass of wine and toast yourself for surviving.

Try this tasty and easy recipe (we all need easy when life is going a little left), and drink a glass or two—or even three!—of Bonterra Cabernet.

Bonterra's Cabernet traditionally offers aromas of Bing cherry, currants and raspberry, with spicy notes of cedar and dried cranberry, with slight vanilla notes. In the glass you'll find juicy red berry flavors, and a very approachable, rich and full mouthfeel with a lingering, thoughtful finish. Good structure, polished yet soft tannins promise an ever more pleasing wine to come, with lively acidity and subtle spice. Biodynamic fruit from McNab and Butler ranches are featured, along with top lots from the finest Mendocino vineyards. This is a Cabernet which will continue to evolve and remain enjoyable for quite some time to come. Please enjoy Bonterra's Good Earth approach.

What to eat with such a great wine? Grilled pork loin in a sundried cherry Cabernet sauce!

GRILLED PORK TENDERLOIN, SUN-DRIED CHERRY & CABERNET GLAZE, CHANTERELLE MUSHROOMS, FINGERLING POTATOES

2 lb. Pork tenderloin
Salt
Pepper
Sugar
2 tbsp vegetable oil
1 bottle Cabernet wine
1½ cups sun dried cherries
Salt and pepper as needed

4 tbsp butter
5 slices bacon (medium dice)
1 large Spanish onion (medium dice)
2 lb Fingerling potatoes (sliced on bias ½ inch thick)
2 tbsp chopped parsley
1 tbsp chopped rosemary
3 Shallots (cut off stems and julienne thinly)
*1 lb Chanterelle mushrooms (pull apart with fingers
   if large)*
2 tbsp chopped fresh thyme

Preheat oven to 350 degrees.

Season pork with salt, pepper, and sugar and sear in a heated sauté pan with vegetable oil. Sear all sides and then place in the oven and cook until the internal temperature reaches 110 degrees. Remove from the oven and let rest for 5 minutes and then slice.

In a saucepan, heat the wine and cherries and bring to a simmer. Reduce by ¼ and then season with salt and pepper. Stir in 2 tablespoons of the butter until incorporated.

Using a separate sauté pan, cook bacon until ¾ of the way cooked and then add onions and potatoes. Cook until potatoes are tender and have a nice crispy outside. Fold in the parsley and rosemary and season with salt and pepper.

In a separate pan, sauté shallots and chanterelles with 2 tablespoons of the butter. Season with salt and pepper and then toss in the thyme.

To serve: Place potatoes in the center of plate. Arrange slices of the pork around the outside, place mushroom mixture on top of potatoes, and spoon cherry sauce over pork. Garnish with a sprig of rosemary.

Four

SIMON had made it a new ritual to join Nikki for coffee before seven every morning. He'd bring Violet with him, and she'd eat her breakfast and watch *Sesame Street*. Times had changed, and, if Nikki admitted it, so had Simon.Violet was his life. The little girl was not lacking at all, because Daddy Simon made sure she had everything a two-year-old princess could ever want. Nikki warned him that in a decade or so his spoiling could come back to bite him. But he didn't seem to think Violet would ever become a hormonal teenager. Nikki tended to disagree.

Marco ran the spa at Malveaux, so Simon was busy being the stay-at-home parent. The arrangement worked out beautifully, and Nikki was overjoyed to see her two best friends settled and happy. Violet had been the blessing Nikki and Derek hoped she'd be, and now they were hoping for a little blessing of their own.

"You loving the hair, or what, girlfriend? You're over

your little tizzy, right, because I almost *so* did not come visit you this morning. I was praying you'd retracted the claws." Simon picked up his coffee cup.

She flashed him her best fake smile. "I love it." She hissed at him and brought her hands up in the shape of claws.

"Your hair is brilliant. You look stunning and everyone in that church is going to think you look stunning as well. Now finish up the coffee, Miss Soon To Be Walking Down The Aisle, and let's go and get your nails done. They look atrocious. Ooh, and don't do that hissing claw thing ever again. Creepy."

Nikki looked at her hands. Doing her nails was not something she did on a regular basis. She found it tedious, but Simon did make a good point. They were stubby and needed some care. "I can't. I have to take Derek's *friends* on a tour around the winery first."

Simon pouted. "Hmmm. Me thinky you not too happy about that."

She pointed at him. "You thinky right."

"So who has shown up so far for the wedding of the century?" Nikki told him. "Ah. Yes, the frat boys and their sorority girls have arrived. I see the dilemma, especially Tristan's other half."

"Savannah? Yeah, what is her deal? She's a world class bi—"

Simon brought his hand up to stop her and pointed at Violet. "Listen up, if you wanna be a mama, you need to clean up that mouth of yours. Maybe I should wash it out with some soap."

"Sorry, but the woman is not nice, and she did not have a problem being rude to me. And get this, that party boy Kenny, who I just don't like at all, why Derek is still friends with him . . ." She shrugged. "Well, last night when we came back from dinner—without Savannah, who had begged off, claiming a migraine—the two of them were lounging in the pool, having drinks. And I think those two were up to no good. She just seemed a little too defensive of that Kenny guy and a little too interested in him."

"Interesting. But you have no time for snooping through the lives of the boring and moronic, and for once murder seems to be escaping you, so let's go with that."

Nikki frowned. "So, do you know anything about Savannah? You did call her boorish and a moron. Interesting terminology."

"No." He looked away.

"You are so lying to me. Simon. Spill."

He brought his hands to his chest and gave her his totally offended look. "I am so not lying."

"Yes, you so are. Why? What do you know? You better tell me. You're going to tell me. I am Violet's godmother."

"Oh, sure, go and involve the baby, why don't you! Why don't you twist the knife and guilt me a little more, Snow White? Hmm, I do miss the dark hair, but I can't go back to calling you Goldilocks. You need some locks for that. We need a new tag, babe, a new nickname for you."

"Simon!"

"Okay, fine. I don't want to tell you this because you are only going to get yourself all worked up and be all anxious, and you are getting married this weekend, but whatever. Savannah has always had a thing for my brother, or at least she did. I don't think Tristan knows, but Derek told me once a few years ago, before you came here, when Derek was married to that psycho piece of work, that Savannah tried to hit on him." Nikki's eyes widened. "See, now don't do that. Do not do that! Don't freak out. You're going to freak out on me, aren't you?"

"I'm not going to freak out on you. I am not. I promise, but there's more to it, isn't there? What aren't you telling me? You've already spilled, now spill the rest. Maybe I'll let you wear the tails. Maybe."

He sighed. "You're ruthless. Derek is going to kill me. Okay. When they were in college, Savannah chased after Derek for a long time, and he repeatedly turned her down. One night, drunk and stupid, he kind of . . ."

"He slept with her?" she shrieked.

Violet stopped banging on her Winnie-the-Pooh piano and turned around, a frown on her face.

"The baby, Nikki. No, he didn't sleep with her, but she kissed him in a drunken stupor. He didn't fall for her slutty little antic. She was already dating Tristan, who was totally in love with her."

"Oh my God." She couldn't help wondering if Derek had kissed Savannah back, way back when. Yes, it was immature and childish, and jealousy was not a good thing, but she still couldn't help herself.

"Now, Nikki, this was twenty-some years ago. You cannot get yourself worked up over this. You can't. My brother loves you. He is a great guy and so he kissed the wrong girl a bazillion years ago and trust me he can't stand her any more than you can."

"I don't even know what to say right now. Sure I get it, sort of, I mean college kids party and make stupid mistakes, but what I don't get is why is he still friends with these people? Particularly Tristan and Savannah?"

"You know Derek. He's a good guy. He never wanted Tristan to know about that incident, and he really felt like Savannah had matured and was in love with Tristan."

"But then when they came out here, what five, six years ago, she hit on him again? Why wouldn't he tell Tristan then what a jerk his wife is?"

"Sure. How do you propose he do that? They have two children. Derek lost his mom and saw what it was like to have a stepmother. My mother. Speaking of, I heard from her the other day."

"I don't care. She's the least of my worries. I'm more bothered by this information. I have to work this through my brain."

"No, you don't. You have to get ready to get married."

That feeling she'd had the night before, the one that made her feel nauseous, traveled through her again.

As she started to say something else, loud honks from a car barreling up the road and past the house echoed off the golden hills and into the valley of grapes. Nikki's stomach twisted. "Who in the world?" She peered out the window and spotted a sleek black Lamborghini. Her stomach sank.

Simon frowned. "I was just getting to that. Remember how I was saying that my mother called the other day?"

"Oh no. No. Please don't tell me. No. That's my worst. Well, one of my worst nightmares come true. Your mother can't be back here. She is not here. Tell me she's not here. Simon, please tell me that. That wasn't her, right?"

Simon closed his eyes, color drained from his face, and the grim expression he wore gave her the answer.

Patrice Malveaux was back on the vineyard.

Five

EVERYTHING about Patrice made Nikki cringe. She was arrogant, self-centered, manipulative, and plain mean. Nikki had hoped and prayed she'd be gone forever. The last she'd heard, Patrice was back in her homeland of Greece and living large off of the inheritance that Derek and Simon's father had left her.

Nikki stared hard at Simon who looked away. "Why is she here?"

Simon closed his eyes. "She's Violet's grandmother, and she wanted to see the baby."

"Bullshit," Nikki said.

Simon's eyes widened. "Nikki!"

"Sorry. I don't think I just harmed the baby. You are not letting my goddaughter go anywhere near that witch."

"Nikki, she is my mother. I know she's dreadful, but people do change."

Nikki rolled her eyes at him. "I don't believe this. I seriously do not believe this. After what that woman put me through, that you would actually defend her? Mother or not, she's evil. It's not like she was June Cleaver to you."

"Nikki—"

"Don't try to reason with me. I know that's what you're going to try to do. And she came back here to ruin my wedding. This has nothing to do with her wanting to get to know her new grandchild. If I had to stake my life on it, I'd bet the idea of being a grandma makes her cringe. She is up to no good." Simon frowned. "You know that I'm right. I find the timing absolutely perfect for her and miserable for me, and I can tell by looking at you that you agree with me."

"I-I-I don't know what to say."

"What can you say? Just do what I ask and keep her far away from me. I now have to go and play hostess to people I don't like, including some one-night stand my fiancé once had."

"He didn't sleep with her."

Nikki walked out the door, almost slamming it, but then remembered Violet inside and decided to keep as much of her cool as she could.

And cool she remained as she approached Derek, who was seated at the large breakfast table at the hotel restaurant with his friends. "Hi, honey, what took you so long? We were waiting. I went ahead and ordered the stuffed French toast for you. I know it's your favorite."

"Wouldn't be mine," Savannah chimed in. "I'm sure it's loaded with calories, and I don't think I'd be wanting to eat too much before my big day."

"Do you always say whatever is on your mind? Or *do* whatever you feel?" Nikki said sitting down.

All eyes turned to her. "Honey, I don't think Savannah meant anything."

"No, I didn't," Savannah said. "I just meant that it wouldn't be my choice. I like eggs."

"Sure." Nikki smiled. She leaned over and kissed Derek's cheek. "Sorry. Wedding jitters. You know all the planning and, um, did you know that Patrice is back?"

"What? Here?"

Nikki nodded. "Here."

"Oh, Patrice. I love her," Savannah said. "When Nancy and Zach came out with us to see you and Mer—I mean before Mer went a little bonkers—Patrice was such a darling hostess, so conscientious. Right Zach?"

Zach didn't reply but took a sip from his coffee cup. Nikki noticed that Tristan bumped Savannah hard on the shoulder.

"You would love Patrice. Can you excuse me? I need to head to the lady's room. I'll be right back. And the French toast is perfect. I'm fortunate to have one of those fast metabolisms."

Nikki headed to the bathroom knowing she should've kept her mouth shut, but that wench had some nerve. This was not what she'd thought the week of her wedding would be like. She didn't really have to use the restroom, but rather needed a minute to get her bearings together. While she was washing her hands, Savannah walked in.

"Nikki, I'm so sorry if I offended you."

Nikki sighed. Comebacks were not one of her strong

suits. She always tried to be a rational, nice, bite-her-tongue kind of gal, but that wasn't going to happen this time. Simon's revelations alone about Savannah made her want to let this woman know exactly what she thought of her and that she was totally on to her. "Actually Savannah, you've been offending me ever since you introduced yourself. Considering the way you've behaved, your apology is a bit unconvincing."

"What?" She brought her hands up to her chest.

"Yep. You have not once been nice to me in the past twenty-four hours. You've actually gone out of your way to be rude to me." Nikki took a step toward the woman who took a step backward. "I'm on to you. I know all about you and what you're really after and you disgust me. Here's the deal, lady. This is my week. *My* wedding week, and you are not going to ruin it with your snide remarks. I'm going to let you stay here *only* because your husband seems nice enough and because my fiancé is friends with him. But you need to stay away from me. Got it. Don't talk to me and if you make one more mean, condescending, awful remark, suggestion, whatever . . ." Nikki took another step toward Savannah, whose eyes widened as she took another step backward leaving her angled up against the stall door. "I will have you escorted off the Malveaux property, and you will never be welcome back here."

Savannah laughed. "Please. Derek would never allow that."

"I don't think my husband-to-be would have any problem with it, actually. And I don't think you want to test my theory. Do you?"

"Everything okay in here?" It was Jackson's wife, Lily.

Nikki turned around with a quaking Savannah behind her. "Peachy keen. Right, Savannah?"

"Perfect," Savanna replied.

"Good. Well the food is here, so the guys thought we should eat and get a move on. I know you have a busy day ahead of you, Nikki. If you need anything, let me know."

"Thank you."

The rest of breakfast went off without a hitch. Savannah barely spoke, and everyone quizzed Nikki and Derek on the wedding details. Nikki tried not to be a phony, but Derek's friends were hard to be real around, and it troubled her that this was his crew. In a way, she felt bad for confronting Savannah the way she had, but the woman did need a lesson in couth and kindness, and although she hadn't delivered it in the nicest way, Nikki wasn't about to let anything worse happen this week. She'd had enough, between the hair, the friends, and Patrice (who she knew would be another chapter of fun and games this week). For now, she tried hard to focus on the tour around the vineyard.

Another thing she was having a hard time with was actually having warm and fuzzy feelings toward Derek. They had to have a talk about Savannah. The kiss she could get over. She knew it was childish to be jealous over something that happened years ago. It did still kind of sting though. And according to Simon, Savannah had been flirtatious toward Derek only a few years ago when she and Tristan had visited. Meredith had been Derek's wife at the time and there was that rule that everyone knew—don't mess with a married man. More so than all of the past issues that had popped up, Nikki realized that most of her anger toward Savannah was because the woman had been rude and obnoxious toward her, and Derek had not exactly defended of her. She would have thought at the breakfast table that he would have said something to give Miss Uppity her comeuppance.

Derek wrapped an arm around her when they were inside the warehouse where the vats were stored. A half dozen large, metal, round tanks fermented grapes into wine, prior to barreling them. The warehouse was chilled, dark and had a cement floor. Particles could be seen floating through the air as a ray of sunshine came through one of the small windows at the top of the warehouse. It smelled of fruit and alcohol.

As she looked over at Savannah who was coldly staring at her, Nikki couldn't help but shrink away, thinking, *that is a woman Derek once kissed*. Jealousy was such an ugly emotion, and Nikki hated feeling it at any level.

"So those things are filled with wine?" Kenny asked.

"You got it. These are all 1200-gallon tanks. After stemming and crushing the grapes, the juice is put into the vats, where alcoholic fermentation takes place. It's the conversion of sugar into alcohol and carbon dioxide. After this, the wine is ready to be barreled and aged," Derek said.

"Now that sounds like a party. Just open up one of those things and everyone drink up."

Derek laughed. "I don't think so. It's not exactly wine yet."

"It's alcohol though, right?" Kenny said.

Lily rolled her eyes. "When are you ever going to grow up, Ken?"

"Never. Why would I want to do that? It doesn't sound like any fun. I like women, wine, and wicked fun." He laughed.

Tristan slapped him on the back. "Not one to change. That's what we love about you."

Nikki thought she might throw up right there on the spot. She also wondered if anyone picked up on the slight sarcasm in Tristan's voice.

"The fumes alone though would kill you. We take measures to make sure no one gets locked inside an empty one. There have been a handful of deaths that way in the area over the years. It's vital to wear the proper equipment."

"I don't think that would be the worst way to go," Kenny said.

"Suffocation?" Lily said. "You think that's cool, huh, Ken?"

Kenny gave her a surprised look and so did her husband. "God, *Lil*, when did you get to be such a . . . I don't know . . . ?"

"What? Bitch? Is that what you were going to call me?" Lily asked.

Now this was amusing. Nikki knew she should feel slightly uncomfortable, but she really didn't.

"Hey, everyone," Derek said. "Come on."

"No, of course I don't mean bitch. I'm sorry, Lily. Maybe I should grow up a bit."

"Maybe you should."

Okay, there was definitely a story here. Nikki knew

that the kind of resentment that Lily showed toward Kenny did not simply come from her thinking his behavior was juvenile. Granted it was, but still . . .

As they walked out of the vat room and started down the pathway to the vines, Nikki noticed Jackson and Lily speaking in hushed tones—the angry kind. Why should she care? She didn't. Not really, but all of the drama had taken her mind off of Patrice.

Walking through the Chardonnay grapes with a suddenly subdued group, Nikki's cell rang. It was her aunt. "Aunt Cara. Hi. You're here?" she asked excitedly. First good thing to happen all week. Derek put an arm around her and she smiled up at him. "What? No. I . . . Ooh my God. That's terrible. When? Okay. Yes. Yes. Of course I understand. I love you, too. Okay. Bye."

"What is it?" Derek asked.

She swallowed back the emotion and tried hard not to cry. "Aunt Cara can't make it. She tripped over her boyfriend's teacup poodle last night and fell against their nightstand. She broke her leg in three places. And her wrist. She has to have surgery on her wrist in a few days, after the swelling goes down."

"Oh, honey."

"I can't believe this. I have to go back to the house."

"I'll come with you."

"No. Finish with your friends. I need some time alone."

"You sure?"

She nodded and hugged him. Walking back down to the house, she knew this all had to be a sign. Maybe this was the wedding that was not supposed to happen. Now tears did blur her vision, and then her text messaging rang. She read the message from a blocked number and turned her face heavenward. "You have to be kidding me." The message read, *Do you believe in fate? MAT.*

Stuffed French Toast and Mimosas

Maybe Nikki should be watching that waist of hers, but stuffed French toast is one of those scrumptious meals that is too difficult to pass up. Plus, there is no better way to take the edge off when people are being just plain icky and rotten than digging into this delightful morning treat. A mimosa is the perfect match for this specialty breakfast.

> *1¼ cups sliced strawberries*
> *½ cup of sugar*
> *1 teaspoon brandy*
> *¼ cup grated orange peel*
> *4 eggs*
> *2 cups heavy whipping cream*
> *1 tbsp brandy*
> *1 tbsp brown sugar*
> *1 tsp vanilla extract*
> *12 slices of egg bread or brioche (thickly cut)*
> *1 tbsp butter*
> *8 tsp mascarpone cream*
> *Powdered sugar*
> *Butter*
> *Maple syrup*

In bowl, mix strawberries, sugar, brandy and orange peel. Let it sit for 30 minutes.

For French toast, beat eggs in medium bowl. Add the cream, sugar, vanilla and brandy. Soak bread in egg mixture. Melt butter on griddle and place bread on and cook for about 4 minutes on each side. Remove from griddle and spread 2 teaspoons mascarpone cream and ¼ cup strawberry mixture in middle and fold in half until cheese melts and strawberries warm up. Sprinkle with powdered sugar and serve with butter and syrup. Pour mimosas.

Six

BY the time Nikki had made it back to the house, anger had taken over. *Do you believe in fate?* She'd deleted the stupid text. What the hell? There were a handful of people who would love to throw a kink into the Sands/Malveaux wedding. Nikki could think of a few in just a matter of seconds—people who might find pleasure in having Nikki all riled up and feeling on edge just two days before her nuptials, as if she needed any more things to set her off. Well, she wasn't going to let any of that get to her. She stood up straight and marched down the cobblestone pathway that led to their front porch, more determined than ever to marry the man of her dreams. Then she stopped dead in her tracks.

Sitting on the porch swing was one of those people who would love to put a kink into the week of wedding festivities. "Patrice," Nikki said, void of any emotion.

Simon's mother stood. She hadn't changed much—

still with the taut face that had been exposed to too much plastic surgery, the fake fingernails that reminded Nikki of claws, the designer outfit over nips and tucks that gave the seventy-year-old woman the body of a thirty-year-old, and, of course, the blond hair that underneath the pale gold color was surely white. Patrice brought her hand up to a diamond cross hanging from her neck. "Hello, Nicole."

"Nikki."

"Yes. It's so nice to see you."

Nikki took a step back. Where the hell was Ollie? Probably asleep in her and Derek's bed. Some watchdog. Who knew how long the old wench had been sitting outside just waiting to get under Nikki's skin. Surely Patrice's visit wasn't a call of congeniality and graciousness. "Really? Nice to see me? Come on. I wish I could say the same thing, but let's be real here, you don't like me and I don't like you. At all."

Patrice's lips eased into a tight smile. "Darling, can't we let bygones be bygones? We are, after all, about to be family. And I adore the new look. It's so much more Napa Valley chic than that mousy look you had before."

Nikki shook her head. "I really don't know why you're here. I mean, I can guess. A few reasons. One, you want the winery or the estate or something, and you see my marriage to your stepson as a problem, because I know that you think this should all be yours, but that wasn't the deal."

Patrice crossed her arms in front of her. "Yes well, the deal is that I do still own a quarter of the winery, along with the main house."

"Great. Then I think we should discuss buying you

out. Face it, you don't want to be here any more than
Derek and I want you here, and I doubt that even your
own son wants you close by. I believe his pet name for
you is 'Mommy Dearest.' "

"Oh, dear." She clucked her tongue. "You may be
mistaken. I've had a nice conversation with my son this
morning, and had a wonderful time with my grand-
daughter, and I believe that Simon has no issue with me
being close by. In fact, seeing that I own the villa on the
hill, I have decided that I am going to be moving back
into it. Simon and Marco and Violet can stay as long as
they like until they find other accommodations. You see,
I need a new home, and I so love the wine country. I've
missed it. I feel home again, and my new husband absolutely adores it."

Nikki balled up her palms. "New husband?" Oh boy,
the writing was on the wall. This was all becoming just
a little too clear for Nikki.

"Yes. You'll get to meet him at your rehearsal dinner.
He's adorable. He's actually tanning himself by the pool
up at the main house. My house."

Nikki sighed. "Patrice, you're not invited to my wedding and you are not invited to our rehearsal dinner."

"Let me be frank. No matter what you think or say,
we are about to be family, and yes, I do know that I have
caused you some problems in the past. I am truly sorry
for that. I had no control over Meredith, and what she
and Cal tried to do to you and Derek. I didn't know they
were cold-blooded murderers. I really didn't." Patrice's
eyes teared up.

This could not be for real. "Whether or not you knew
they were killers, you were all gung ho for Meredith to

try to win back Derek, get pregnant so there was an heir. Then, because she was your daughter, a fact which, let me remind you, no one knew but you, you and Meredith would have had control over the estate and the winery. But that didn't happen because your daughter lost her marbles and planned to kill Derek and me, too. So, this sob act you have going? I'm not buying it."

"I've changed. I really have, and I think in all fairness you should give me the chance to prove it. I'm Violet's grandmother and you're her godmother. Can't we move forward, forget the past? It's fate that we've been brought together as a family." She rubbed the cross again around her neck.

"What did you say?" Nikki asked.

"Let's forget the past."

"No, about fate?"

"That we should be a family."

Nikki glared at her for a second, then turned around and unlocked her front door. Once inside she turned back around before slamming it in Patrice's face, yelling, "Fate nothing. We will never be family. You and me. Never. And you are not coming to my wedding."

Hands shaking, Nikki went to her bedroom and changed quickly into a pair of shorts and T-shirt, and put on her running shoes. She glanced over at the bed and, sure enough, the Ridgeback was spread out across it, half the covers on him. Ollie had a knack for pushing and pulling on the covers until he had them the way he liked them. His head rested on Nikki's pillow. She smacked him lightly on the butt. "Get your ass up, you lazy bum. We're going for a run." Usually not much got Ollie moving, but he did like the jogs they took, so he pricked his ears and lifted his head. Nikki laced her shoes and stood up. "Let's go, watchdog of the year." Ollie jumped off the bed. Nikki grabbed his leash because she planned to take an extra long run and go on into town where she'd need the leash. She may not really have had the luxury of spare time, since there were preparations to check off for the big day, including the final fitting on her wedding gown, but at that moment all she wanted to do was get outside and run away from all of it.

And that's what she did.

Nikki and Ollie took off down the dirt road, kicking up dust behind them. Chaparral and grape vines lined the pathways. She ran hard and fast, the colors of the early summer months in the wine valley all bleeding in together—shades of pale gold to mustard seed yellow, sand to mahogany soil, grapes the colors of palm fronds and deep purple, and overhead the sky was bright blue with a scatter of fluffy clouds here and there. The smells were a heavenly brew of wine, oak, olive, and something sweet and wild—maybe orange blossoms. It was why she ran like this. The colors, the smells, the sounds of birds singing and her feet pounding against the hard dirt, and her dog chasing after every rabbit— never catching one—melted all the crap away. At least for those moments. All the stress and anxiety—the hair, Derek's friends, Patrice, Aunt Cara not coming to the wedding, the stupid note and text from some creep who called himself Moros Apate Thanatos—she knew she still had to look up the meaning of that, but there was so much going on, so much to handle she'd barely found a minute to breathe. Taking this run with the dog was something she knew would calm her and help her think clearly. She was right, as the negative feelings seemed to dissipate in the warm summer breeze that floated down from the hills of Napa and into the valley.

Nikki and Ollie ran until they came into the little town of Yountville. She thought about going in and seeing if Isabel would talk to her. Isabel's restaurant Grapes was in Yountville, and Nikki had spent plenty of time there with Isabel and Andrés, eating good food, drinking good wine, and spending time with great company. But those days were behind her, and she knew she should let them go and leave Isabel alone.

They walked along the sidewalk, Ollie huffing and puffing away. She ducked into a store and bought a couple of large waters, and took Ollie to the quaint park area where she sat down on a bench and poured several handfuls of water into her palms for Ollie to drink from. Once he had his fill, she pounded her water and leaned back, closing her eyes and soaking in the sun. Ollie lay down at her feet, and they both daydreamed for a few minutes, until Nikki heard her name. Startled she opened her eyes. Shocked, she couldn't speak. Before her stood Andrés Fernandez.

Seven

"ANDRÉS. Oh my gosh. Hi. I didn't know you were in town."

"Yes. I came back a couple of days ago. I have business here to take care of, and I wanted to see my sister. Your hair. It's nice. Very pretty on you," he said, his Spanish accent rolling off his tongue.

A flood of memories of times they'd spent together ran through Nikki's mind.

She brought her hands up to the tips of her hair above her ears. "Thank you. You look great. And business is good with the winery in Spain?" And he did look great. That was no lie. Andrés had always been a handsome man with olive skin and dark eyes with lashes that were so thick they almost didn't look real.

"The winery is good. Grapes are planted and in a few years we should have our first harvest, but I had always promised the winery here that I would come back and make wines for them until my first harvest is ready. I'll have to go back at times to make sure everything is working fine, but I have good people working for me. And you? How are you? I hear you're getting married."

She shifted a little on the bench. "I am. Yes. Actually in two days."

"Oh. Soon. Good for you. I think you and Derek will be happy together. I always thought that we would be happy together, too. But you once told me that the heart knows what the heart wants, and your heart didn't want mine."

Why didn't he just take out a knife, stab it in her heart and twist at that moment. "I'm sorry. You know that I am. I thought we were okay. That you were okay."

"I am, and you have no need to feel sorry. I have moved on."

Those words *moved on* tugged at her a little bit and she wished they didn't. "Good. So you're seeing someone?"

"Maybe. I had a friend in Spain. She was lovely but not the one I wanted to finally make a life with. And I think you know that ultimately that's what I'm looking for."

"Yes. But then what's this maybe all about, if the woman in Spain isn't exactly what you want?"

He pointed to the bench. "May I?"

"Of course." Why was it that things between two people who had once deeply cared about one another—and if the truth were told, they still cared about one another, it was simply that the way they cared had changed— could be so awkward in the way they communicated and acted around each other afterward? It was always like that with breakups. Even with people who didn't

have bad breakups. Nikki wished it wasn't like that.
But she couldn't deny that she was happy to see him.
There was something about him still that made her feel
at ease, almost peaceful. The camaraderie between them
had never been the problem. The chemistry, for Nikki at
times, had.

He sat down. "I see you still like to run with your
sidekick." He scratched Ollie between the ears.

"He's definitely my pal. I think he missed you."

He smiled. "I missed him."

"So tell me what's going on." Nikki didn't want to
walk down memory lane with him. She was afraid of the
turmoil it might cause.

"Actually there is this woman, and you know her."

Nikki felt her eyebrows shoot up. "I do?"

Andrés nodded. "Yes. See, she contacted me about
a month ago, and we've been e-mailing each other back
and forth about some ideas."

"Ideas. What kind of ideas? Who is it? You said that
it was someone that I knew."

"Oh, well, there she is now. We're planning on having
lunch." He pointed across the street to where an amazing looking woman sat—all golden and toned. Totally
one of those women that all other women hate because
she's *that* gorgeous and men love because she's *that*
gorgeous.

Nikki recognized the woman and the convertible,
a silver blue BMW, immediately. Renee Rothschild.
"Renee? You're interested in her?" Of course he was.
Most men, all men, including Nikki's man, had at one
time or another been interested in Renee.

Renee Rothschild's father owned a publishing house

in San Francisco where Renee was the editor-in-chief. She also wrote a gossip-type column that was syndicated in newspapers on the West Coast. A couple of years back, Renee had been working on a cookbook with a chef who worked at Malveaux, but then the chef was tragically murdered. At the time, Renee decided it would be brilliant to do a book with Derek on wineries and spas and wanted to showcase the Malveaux Winery and Spa in the book. What she really wanted to do was get Derek in the sack, and she'd come awfully damn close. She'd even almost gone to Australia with Derek, who at the last moment changed his mind and asked Nikki to go.

Now what did she want with Andrés? And why was it upsetting Nikki to know that Andrés was interested in her?

"I do like her. We haven't really had any dates, only back and forth with the e-mail. She's working on a book about international winemakers, and she wants me to be the focus, I guess."

"Of course." Modus operandi hadn't changed for Renee.

Andrés called out to her and waved at her. As Renee sauntered over, Nikki tried hard not to run away. Maybe Renee wouldn't recognize her with the new 'do.' She was surprised that Andrés had, especially with her eyes closed.

"Oh, my goodness. Nikki, how nice to see you. I love your hair," Renee said. "Glamorous. What are you doing here? Don't you have a wedding to get ready for? I saw you and Derek in the paper."

"Yes. I was out getting a little exercise with Ollie. I stopped for a rest, and Andrés found me here."

"Ah, fate," Renee said. "Nice."

Nikki cringed, and Ollie lifted his head and growled. He'd never liked Renee. "Yes. Fate. I better be getting back, and you two better be working on that book. Andrés, please tell your sister hello. I miss her."

"I will do that."

Nikki put Ollie on the leash, and they started back toward the winery with Renee's interesting choice of word ringing in her ears.

Eight

COULD anyone have a stranger couple of days leading up to their wedding? Not only had all the crazy stuff happened, but now it seemed like all the ghosts of Nikki's past were coming back to haunt her. First Patrice and now Andrés and Renee. The even stranger part was that two out of three of the ghosts from Nikki's past had both used the word "fate" when speaking to her.

She knew it was likely just a coincidence, but was it? What was Renee's deal with Andrés? Did she just like to go after men that Nikki dated? Or, again—coincidence?

There was no time to ponder it at all. She was officially running late after taking her late morning run. She'd had to reschedule the nail appointment Simon insisted on, and then she'd had to pick up her dress and call the caterers to make sure they added two vegetarian plates, as a couple of late replies had just come in. She then made it by the florists to drop off the final payment, and then she ran by the drugstore to pick up a few items—like new mascara and some eyeliner.

Planning their wedding had been quite a large undertaking. At first they'd agreed that smaller was better, and Derek helped as much as he could. Simon had really stepped in where he was needed, loving every second of playing wedding planner. He had much better design and fashion sense than Nikki did, so she pretty much allowed him to take over. The cake he'd chosen was five times more beautiful than any Nikki might have picked—lemon with raspberry cream, the top decorated with miniature rosebuds and plumeria. He just had that flair, and she was grateful that he did.

The problem was that the idea of a small wedding had gotten way out of hand. Although Nikki only had Simon and Alyssa standing up for her, and Derek only had Marco and Jonah, the guest list wasn't reflective of the tiny wedding party. It seemed that Derek knew virtually everyone in Napa and Sonoma Counties, and almost everyone was important in some way to him or the business. By the time the final count had come in, they were expecting almost four hundred guests. Nikki felt that this was about three hundred and fifty too many, but what had gotten out of hand was now too late to rein in, so she was going to make do. Her focus needed to be on her groom and her day and not all of the people who would be attending.

And at that moment she needed to get ready and be out the door for the rehearsal. Thankfully, it would be only the immediate wedding party at the church. Their *friends* would be joining them for the dinner afterward that was being held at the vineyard restaurant.

Simon had picked out a gorgeous azure blue dress that was off the shoulder and draped down the front—chiffon and silk. It was shorter than Nikki normally would have chosen, but Simon insisted it showed off her legs, which he also insisted were one of her best features. She wasn't too sure about that, but as with anything Simon insisted upon, she'd learned to nod her head in agreement and go with it.

Nikki leaned into her BFF at the rehearsal while the minister was walking Derek, Marco, and Jonah through their motions. Alyssa was on the other side of Nikki on the phone with the babysitter. "Where's Violet?"

Simon bit his lower lip.

Nikki tilted her head. "Simon? Where is Violet? Who's she with?"

He looked up at the ceiling of the church rafters. Of course, to accommodate all of the people who would be coming to the wedding the following afternoon, they'd had to choose a large church—St. Luke's. It was Episcopal, which was the denomination Derek had grown up with. Nikki had started attending recently. Even though the candlelight in the church bounced gently off of a stained glass image of the Virgin Mary, Nikki felt like she was about to strangle Simon, because she knew the answers to where and with whom Violet was.

"She's with Patrice, isn't she? How could you?"

The pastor and the guys looked over at her. "Everything okay?" Derek asked.

"Of course," she said. Simon was wringing his hands. "How could you?" she whispered. "How could you trust that woman?"

Alyssa hung up the phone and leaned in, her hazel

eyes shining with amusement. "I have a feeling I'm about to be entertained."

Simon gave her the evil eye.

Nikki patted her hand. "I may need backup, sister. Or, actually, you may have to hold me back from murdering him."

"Stop it. Stop being so impossible. She's my mother, and she begged me. Try to understand."

Nikki had no understanding whatsoever. Her own mother had completely abandoned her as a child and not once had she ever thought to pick up the phone, reach out and trust her again—mother or not. "I don't understand." She glanced at Alyssa. "Do you understand?"

Alyssa held up both of her hands. "I'm not getting involved in this."

"I'm sorry. Be rational here. She won't hurt the baby," Simon said.

"I don't think she would. What I think is that she's trying to worm her way back into the family, and it looks to be working. On top of that, I am certain that she has some kind of plan up her sleeve to make sure that this wedding doesn't take place."

Simon's jaw dropped. "Oh, come on now. You are being simply ridiculous." He leaned forward and looked at Alyssa. "She is, isn't she?"

"I told you, I'm out of this. I'm only here to watch the show. Fireworks are happening." Alyssa rubbed her hands together.

Nikki nodded. "Yes, they are. For the past week, I've been receiving these ominous-type messages." She briefly explained.

"Patrice wouldn't do that."

"I don't know," Alyssa commented. "After what Nikki has told me about your mom, no offense, Si, but she doesn't exactly sound like a sweet lady. She sounds kind of vindictive. And signing the notes with Greek names? That's really strange. I think Moros means death. Not sure about the other two."

"Super. I've been meaning to get online and do some detective work, but I really haven't had a lot of time, and I just figured that it was someone trying to freak me out. It would make sense if it was Patrice," Nikki said.

"I don't know. It scares me. I think you need to tell Jonah about all of this." Alyssa faced Nikki, her pretty face slightly drawn, reflecting true fear.

"I honestly haven't put much thought into it. I think someone is having fun at my expense and trying to put my already frazzled bride nerves even more on edge. And who wouldn't love to see me come totally unglued?" She arched her eyebrows at Simon.

He tossed his hands up. "Okay. Maybe she would. I'll snoop around and find out if she's been doing it."

"Better yet, send her on her merry way. Do not encourage her, Simon. She will break your heart. Mother or not. She *will* break your heart. What does Marco say about this? I'm sure he has an opinion."

He looked down at his feet, which he'd started tapping against the hard floor.

"Ah, see, he agrees with me, doesn't he?"

He shrugged.

"Of course he does," Alyssa said. "I'd bet having your mom around puts a little cramp in your life."

"Oh, it's not just his mother who's hanging out at the house. I understand she's found herself a new husband."

Simon nodded, his face darkening. "I think he's younger than me."

"No," Nikki and Alyssa said simultaneously.

"Oh, that is creepy wrong," Alyssa said.

"I can't believe you convinced Marco to leave Violet with her and this new husband of hers. You don't even know him."

"It wasn't easy," he mumbled. "Marco is staying in the hotel until I can get her to go."

"Good for him."

"Nikki!"

"Everything still all right?" the minister asked.

"Yes!" they shouted in unison.

"He asked me to bring Violet over in the evenings so she can stay with him at night."

Nikki didn't reply.

"You've got to fix that, my friend," Alyssa said.

"No kidding. What am I supposed to do?" he asked. "Any ideas from the peanut gallery?"

"I guess only you have the answers to that, but if it were me, I'd find a way to get rid of Mommy Dearest so you, so *we,* can all get our lives back on track. I think sooner rather than later. We all need to get together and come up with a fair offer and buy her out of the house. I mean look at what she's asking of you and Marco."

"Aren't you helpful," he replied. "How about you? Any ideas?" he asked Alyssa.

She shrugged. "No. But I wish you luck."

"Sure, the two of you rib the hell out of me and give orders and make demands, but you have no clue how to help me. Some friends you are." He crossed his arms and let out an aggrieved sigh.

Before Alyssa and Nikki could either come up with something helpful or another smart-ass comment, the minister called the three of them forward.

The rehearsal went off without a hitch, other than Simon's bombshell news about Patrice. On the drive back to the vineyard, Derek took Nikki's hand and held it tight. She sensed an anxiety in him that hadn't been there until that moment. She didn't want to say anything because Simon and Marco were in the backseat, and neither one of them was doing much talking. Nikki doubted that Derek was unaware of the trouble in paradise, or the fact that his step-monster wanted to move back into the main house permanently. She thought about bringing it up at that moment, seeing as how they were all in the car and it might be a good time to come up with a plan. But the tension she felt coming from him made her think that the timing wasn't right. Plus, all she really wanted to do was get back to the restaurant, have a glass of wine, a good dinner, and go to bed. Tomorrow was her day, and she was trying to muster a little more excitement.

The Malveaux restaurant looked more beautiful than ever. This was not a detail Nikki or Simon had taken care of but rather Derek. He'd insisted on planning the entire dinner from the décor to the menu. He hadn't missed a thing. When they walked through the arches into the open patio, one of Nikki's favorite local bands— The Bottlenecks—was playing the instrumental version of "When a Man Loves a Woman," white candles were lit throughout, across tables and in sconces on the patio walls, the fireplace was lit, and there were small clustered bouquets of miniature roses, tuberose, and lilacs on the table—all of Nikki's favorites. "You didn't miss a thing."

"I did my best." He flashed her his brilliant smile, and all of the stress melted way far away. She didn't even glance at Savannah, who was thankfully seated at the end of the table. Simon had gone to the house and picked up Violet, which thrilled Nikki and Marco both. He'd also whispered in Nikki's ear that he planned to talk to Derek, agreeing that she was right. He couldn't allow his mother to just waltz in and try to run the show. Nikki wasn't quite convinced that he was telling her the truth, but for now, she figured buying it would please everyone, including her.

Even Kenny was on his best behavior, and actually told a pretty funny and somewhat charming story about his aging mother who had been walking slowly across the street when some "badass" (Kenny's words) in a BMW decided she wasn't moving fast enough, so he blared his horn at her. Kenny's mom had then taken her purse and banged it on the front of the guy's car, and she did it so hard that his air bag deployed. "Guy was pissed, but my mom just kept on walking while he stood there yelling at her. The best part is, she gets across the street where some teens were, and she gave the guy the finger. The kids loved it. Told her if the dude came near her again, they'd protect her."

The entire table broke out laughing, except for Tristan and Savannah who seemed rather distracted.

The first course was brought out and again, Derek hadn't forgotten a thing. Gambinos with pasilla chile, goat cheese, and crostini. Hmmm. Tasty. With that they opened a bottle of champagne, and the celebrating went on from there. It didn't take long before Nikki realized she might have had more than her share of champagne.

The full meal was absolutely delicious and over the top from the shrimp and crostini, Caesar salad, sea scallops in a pear champagne cream sauce and, for dessert, a crème brûlée.

After dessert and more champagne and laughter, Derek asked Nikki to dance. Others joined in and some watched. Derek kissed her. "I want you to know that I know what a hard few days this has been for you. But I also want you to know that our love can survive anything that comes our way. All of this outside crap that's gone down is only that, outside crap. It doesn't diminish anything we have between us, and nothing and no one can come between us."

"I know." She kissed him back. "It's fate. That's why we're together." God, there was that word again. How had that slipped out?

He pulled away from her slightly and looked at her, an odd expression on his face.

"What's the matter?" she asked.

"Nothing." He shook his head.

"You're lying. That's not a good way to begin our marriage. What is it? What's the matter, Derek?"

He took her by the hand. "Come on."

They said a quick good night, and surely everyone figured that they were going to get an early start on the honeymoon rituals. But Nikki knew that was the furthest thing from Derek's mind. She could tell by the tension in his voice and the way he'd been acting all night.

As they started to leave the restaurant, the host stopped them. "Ms. Sands, a courier dropped this by earlier." He handed her a large envelope. Derek intercepted and grabbed it.

"Derek?"

Once back outside, he tore it open. He pulled out a photo of himself and Renee Rothschild. It was from a newspaper article that had been printed last year when they'd worked on the book project together. In big red, block letters it, of course, read, *Do you believe in fate? Sincerely,* Moros Apate Thanatos.

Derek's face turned red. "Is this the first one you've gotten? The first message?"

Nikki felt her insides shake. "No. I got one with you and Meredith from a newspaper photo, and then I got a text with the same message from a blocked number today."

"For how long? When did you get the first one?"

"About a week ago. Why? What's going on?"

"Let me guess, you didn't want to tell me because you didn't want to worry me or put a damper on our week?"

She nodded.

He nodded, too. "Yep. That's why I didn't want to tell you. I've been getting the same messages."

"Oh my God. I'm sorry I didn't tell you."

He pulled her in close. "I'm sorry that I didn't tell you either. I wanted this to be the best week in the world for you."

"I know. What do you think it means? And what's with the signature?"

"I think someone is trying their damndest to freak us out, but I don't know why. What do you think it means?" he asked.

"That someone out there doesn't want us to get married."

*   *   *

NIKKI isn't exactly a stranger to the odd and mysterious. How she's kept her sanity through her years in Napa Valley is a mystery in and of itself. Or maybe it's all that champagne, wine, and good food that keeps her going through the hard times. It also helps that she has herself a good man. The question is, will their love survive all of this turmoil. Nikki would be a fool to not see how good she's got it. Any man who can come up with the décor and menu for such an important evening is worth hanging on to, even when dangerous forces seem to be at work trying to make certain that these two never tie the knot.

Those sea scallops in that pear cream sauce alone make Derek worth all of the ups and downs.

When it seems you and your loved one may have hit a bump in the road, offer up this delicious meal with Bonterra's 2007 Viognier and soon enough, things will be back on track.

Pan Seared Scallops, Champagne-Pear Cream and Chervil

with Bonterra Viognier

SERVES 4

Following an established Bonterra custom, the winemaker has layered sister White Rhone varietals Marsanne and Roussanne in the blend, adding a dimension of complexity to Bonterra's signature Viognier. Marsanne provides a rich texture and green apple flavor, while Roussanne contributes pear and haunting floral notes. A touch of Muscat adds to the exciting aroma of this wine. The Mediterranean climate of the North Coast, combined with careful selection of the right rootstocks (101-14, 5C, 110R), particularly the aromatic Viognier Clone 642 that does well in the gravelly, loamy soils in the region, brings the exceptional Viognier fruit even in challenging growing seasons. Bonterra followed their usual style of fermenting in both stainless (62%) and barrel (38%), not using malolactic fermentation and leaving the wine in oak for just a moment to gain a note of vanilla. The increasing use of stainless provides ever fresher and decidedly forward fruit that leaps from the glass. Powerful aromas of freshly sliced harvest peach, hints of honeysuckle and an exotic note of jasmine dominate in the glass. Peaches and cream remain a sensory signature of this wine. Complex fruit flavors of apricot and peach are overlaid with notes of oaky vanilla. The wine is crisp yet creamy, a grand alternative to everyday whites. There is balance and elegance. For many, this is a favorite Bonterra offering, and it's easy to see why. This vintage won't disappoint.

1 quart heavy cream
16 large scallops, seasoned with salt and pepper
3 pears, (Bosc or Anjou) sliced thin
2 tsp salt
1½ tsp pepper
1½ tsp sugar
2 tsp ground coriander
¼ cup champagne

4 tbsp
1 bunch chervil
1 tbsp extra virgin olive oil

In a saucepan, reduce cream by half over medium heat and reserve.

Slice pears thinly. Mix salt, pepper, sugar, and coriander together and then toss with the pears. Heat a sauté pan with 2 tablespoons of the butter and cook pears until they caramelize. Add champagne and let cook for approximately 2 minutes, and then add the heavy cream reduction. Finish with salt & pepper and set aside.

Heat another sauté pan. When hot, sear scallops with the rest of the butter and cook until desired temp.

Toss Chervil sprigs in olive oil and salt and pepper.

To plate: Arrange scallops in a circle, place the pear sauce in the center, and drizzle some sauce on the scallops. Garnish with the chervil.

Nine

THE day was finally here, and although the week had been not every bride's dream, Nikki couldn't wait to say "I do" and become Mrs. Malveaux. Then it would be on to the honeymoon, which was a two-week dream vacation, first to Tuscany and then to the Mediterranean coast. That was what she was looking forward to the most. She peered out the small window inside the church dressing room. "It does not look good out there," she said. "Those clouds are awfully dark."

"Not to worry. If it rains, you're in luck," Simon replied, unzipping the bag holding the Badgley Mischka wedding gown.

"In luck? How do you figure?"

"Rain on your wedding day means good luck."

"I don't think so."

"He's right," Alyssa chimed in. "I've heard that, too." She bent down and tied the bow around Violet's light aqua dress. "I can't wait to see Petie. Thank God Jonah is taking care of him."

"Hmmm. Maybe you'll catch the bouquet," Nikki said turning to face Alyssa.

She smiled, a pink blush creeping into her cheeks. "I can't say that I'd mind that at all."

"Someone in love?" Simon asked.

"I am. We are. He just told me, and I told him. I'm sorry, Nikki."

"For what? I think it's wonderful."

"It is. I know. But this is your day."

"Um, and that means what? That I can't share the day with love and everyone who is in love? Please. I'm very happy for you and Jonah. He is a great man."

"He is. And so sweet."

"And so hot," Simon interjected. The women looked at him. He shrugged. They all laughed. "What can I say? I'm honest."

Nikki did like Jonah Robinson, Alyssa's boyfriend. He was a detective with the Sonoma County sherriff's department, and although the two of them had had a difference of opinion more than once, they liked and respected one another. They'd actually solved a murder case together and found they liked working with each other. When Alyssa began dating Jonah, Nikki was a bit concerned because he didn't exactly seem the marrying type, but she'd learned quickly that she was wrong. Jonah had fallen hard for both Alyssa and Petie. They seemed to make a perfect little family together. And Simon wasn't kidding when he'd made the remark about Jonah being hot. He definitely wasn't hard on the eyes. He had a Lenny Kravitz look to him that leant itself to a subdued rock star quality. His sea green eyes stood out against his mocha colored skin. Alyssa and Jonah were the kind of couple that made people on the streets do double takes. Like Jonah, Alyssa was exotic, with long dark hair, hazel eyes, and creamy skin. If they ever had children together, they'd be model pretty. Nikki was sure of that. "I will do my best to aim the bouquet your way."

"Deal. By the way, did you talk to him about those notes with the Greek signature on them?"

"No." Nikki frowned. She didn't want to tell Alyssa that Derek had also been receiving them. Last night when they'd gone home, they'd agreed it was some stupid prank and their wedding day needed to be only about them. That was what they wanted to focus on. Once they were married and on to their honeymoon, all of this nonsense would go away. "It's fine. Believe me. I don't want to discuss it. I want to get married."

"I'm sorry. I'm a little worried is all."

"I'm fine." Nikki gave her a hug. "Really. Promise."

Alyssa smiled at her. "Okay. I believe you. Now hurry and get the dress on. Time is ticking You can't leave the groom waiting. Come on."

Simon picked up Violet. "I'll go and check on the groom, and you'd better be ready when we return."

Simon left the room with Violet, and Alyssa helped Nikki into her gown. Her friend stood back and admired her after zipping up the back of the dress. The Badgley Mischka gown followed the length of Nikki's silhouette, draping over her in silk. It had a sheer top layer of chiffon with tiny crystal beads sewn on about every few inches, giving the dress a shimmering effect. Across the neckline of the strapless beauty was an intricate row of the crystal beads. Alyssa took a step back. "You look amazing. Honestly, I don't think I've ever seen any bride look so beautiful. And that dress!" Her eyes welled up with tears. "You are stunning."

"You're so sweet. Thank you." She gave her friend a hug. "I don't know how I could have done any of this without you. This week has been crazy and you've been a huge help."

"Are you kidding me? I've loved every minute of it."

Nikki smiled at her, but she couldn't help but think of Isabella. She loved Alyssa and was truly thankful for all she'd done for her over the week, not the least of which had been distracting Patrice and keeping Nikki from killing Savannah, but there was this part of her that really wished Isabella was there. She'd never imagined that they wouldn't be friends. But she did understand. Blood was thicker than water, and Nikki had broken her brother's heart. But he seemed fine now. He'd apparently moved on. But with Renee Rothschild? That was such a disconcerting thought.

Alyssa opened up the box that held the veil and took it out, draping it over Nikki's head. It was a simple, long sheath of chiffon, with the same small beads throughout, secured on top of her head with a thin silk band.

Nikki did a twirl and had to admit she felt like a princess. "You ready?" Alyssa asked.

Nikki's stomach sunk. "I think so."

"No more thinking about it. It's now or never."

Nikki slicked on her lip gloss and put her hair back behind her ears—what little hair there was. She was kind of used to it by now. Simon returned and peeked around the door frame, Violet in his arms. "Lord have mercy. You do look rather Princess Grace." He let out a low whistle. "Take my breath away."

"I have something for you," Nikki said. "Take off your jacket," she ordered Simon. She took a garment bag from the small closet in the dressing room and handed it over to him.

"What's this?" he asked. Nikki shrugged. He unzipped the bag and took out his new jacket. "Tails? Oh, you are the best! You're my queen."

Nikki shook a finger at him. "No, I'm not. There's only room for one queen in this wedding, and I don't think I'm it."

Simon smiled. "Good point. You're my princess then."

"I'm good with that."

"I think we'd better head over," Alyssa said. "Time to go." She tapped her watch.

"I think we have a few minutes," Simon said.

Nikki took a quick look at the clock on the wall. "It is time."

"No." He shook his head. "Well, technically it is time. But there are still a lot of people coming into the church."

Nikki peered out the window again. "Parking lot looks full and I don't see but a couple of people heading in."

"Trust me. There are some stragglers. Go powder your nose again. It looks a little shiny."

"I just did it," Nikki replied.

"No, it looks like an oil slick after the *Exxon Valdez* disaster."

Nikki crossed her arms in front of her. "What's the problem, Jay Leno?"

"No problem. Just making sure you're as gorgeous as

can be for this big day of all days to remember—this glorious day filled with love and life and joy. This is a day that will go down in in . . ."

"Simon!"

"What?" He looked at her, eyes wide. Violet laughed. "Oh, see, Daddy make a funny face? Funny face for Auntie Nikki's big day. Yeah. Funny faces. You make a funny face with Daddy, and Aunt Nikki make a funny face, and Alyssa . . . ," he sing-songed.

"Derek isn't here, is he?" Nikki interrupted Simon's silly antics to try to distract her.

He stopped, set Violet down and looked Nikki in the eyes. "No. He isn't. But they are on the way. I know it."

Nikki found herself stuttering. "You know it? What do you know? Are you sure they're on their way? Did you talk to Derek? How do you know for sure?" Her stomach twisted. A horrible feeling came over her. What if he'd changed his mind? What if this was one of those weddings where the groom suddenly changes his mind? Big did it to Carrie. Could Derek do it to Nikki?

A tap at the door and everyone turned to look. Nikki looked at Alyssa who looked at Simon, who went to the door. He cracked it open. All Nikki could hear were whispers from the other side.

Simon gently shut the door and clasped his hands together.

"He doesn't want to marry me, does he?" Nikki asked.

"He's not coming."

Ten

"SHUT your mouth. Of course he wants to marry you. He's waiting for you at the altar right now. Come on, drama queen, let's get this show on the road."

"I could kill you," she whispered as they walked out the door.

"I was just spicing it up for you."

"I've had enough spice already. Thank you very much."

"Enough complaining. Stand tall. Be pretty. Chop-chop."

They turned the corner of the hall in the church and came to the closed doors. Nikki took a deep breath. Aunt Cara was supposed to be here walking her down the aisle. She turned to Simon. "Will you give me away?"

He took a step back. "Oh, honey. Really?"

She nodded. Tears filled both of their eyes.

"Now stop that. We'll mess up our mascara. Then

we'll look like a couple of raccoons. But can I give you
away and be your maid of honor?"

"It's not exactly traditional, but so what? I love you.
You're my best friend and you're going to be my brother
now, so will you give me away?"

"You bet, princess." He kissed her cheek.

Alyssa opened the doors for them. One of the ladies
who worked the front desk at Malveaux came around
and took Violet to go and sit with her. She also had Petie
in tow.

Alyssa started down the aisle. Nikki and Simon
moved into position.

Canon in D by Johann Pachelbel played as the wedding procession started down the aisle. "This is it. And
if I haven't told you before, I am happy to be getting you
for a sister. And as far as a best friend, you sealed that
deal when you let me wear the tails."

"Don't make me laugh." Nikki's stomach was coiled
up in a snake pit of nerves. The guests all stood, and
Nikki and Simon proceeded down the aisle. Going past
all of the people was like a blur—a sea of faces, most
of whom she didn't recognize. The church was packed.
But as soon as she got about halfway down, Nikki's eyes
locked on Derek's and the nerves went away, a smile
spread across her face, and she knew that everything
was going to be right with her world. The church was
filled with stephanotis, the sent of the gorgeous tropical fragrance filled the church, candles were lit, and the
music being played by the cellist seated in the choir loft
resounded off the walls.

They were partially down the aisle when the cellist
stopped playing. Nikki went to take another step. Simon

turned around to look back. A whizzing sound, almost as if a Learjet was flying past her ear, echoed through the church. Simon pushed her into an aisle of guests. Nikki went to lift herself up, but screams and a rush of panic went through the church.

Complete mayhem played out as people ducked down in their pews. Nikki glanced over at Simon who was on the ground. That's when Nikki saw it—blood. Simon's blood. He'd been shot.

Eleven

"OH my God! Oh my God! Simon! Hey, man! Hey, man, talk to me. I'm right here." Derek had bolted over to where Simon had fallen and was kneeling next to him.

Simon's face drained of color, his eyelids fluttering. "I don't feel so good. It hurts. My arm hurts."

Blood stained the arm of the tuxedo and dripped onto the floor. Derek looked up at Nikki, his eyes pleading, but for what she didn't know. It was all surreal, like a big blurry haze, and all she could do was stand there.

Marco was out of breath, leaning over Simon. *"Mi amor. Oh, mio dio!"* Tears filled Marco's eyes. "No, no, no, no! What is happening? How did this . . ."

Nikki laid a hand on Marco's shoulder. She heard people clamoring to get out of the church, and she heard Jonah's voice echoing off the church walls. "No one move! Stay where you are! I'm with the police department! Remain in your seats!" He'd raced up the back stairs to the rectory—to where the shot had come from. A few seconds later he yelled out, "I need paramedics up here, too!"

The cellist. Nikki brought a hand to her mouth to stifle the gasp. The poor woman. Oh, God. Please let her be okay. It had to be her, unless it was the shooter. It dawned on Nikki that whoever had just shot Simon could still be inside the church.

"*Mio dio. Mio dio*," Marco whispered. "He has to be well. He cannot be . . . he has to . . . Simon?"

"Hi, love," Simon whispered back weakly as Marco sat down by his head, stroking his hair. "My arm hurts. It aches," he moaned.

Nikki crouched down next to Simon and took his hand. "Hold still. Help is coming. Okay, sweetie. It's going to be okay." Nikki remembered reading over her Aunt Cara's police procedural manuals and doing research during her acting days for a scene that felt vaguely familiar to what was taking place at this moment. She glanced at Derek. "Can we get the sleeve off of him?"

His eyes wide, Derek began to shake his head. "I don't . . ."

"Look, if he's bleeding a lot, we should do something to stop it. We need to put some kind of pressure on it."

"*Sì!* Yes, we must do that. Stop his bleeding," Marco said.

Tristan had come over next to them. "I have a pocket knife," he said.

"In your tux?" Nikki asked.

He shrugged. "Swiss Army. It's, uh, it was a gift. Sentimental."

"Who the hell cares? Let me have it," Derek ordered.

Tristan handed him the knife, and Derek gently cut the sleeve off of his brother's arm.

It didn't appear that the bullet was lodged anywhere in Simon's arm, but a decent part of his upper bicep was torn away and still bleeding. Nikki took off her veil and wrapped it tightly around his arm in hopes of stopping the bleeding.

"Princess, no! Not the veil. God, no! It's a Badgley Mischka for God's sakes. What are you thinking?" Simon slurred.

"Be quiet and just relax, okay? It's fine."

"It hurts," he moaned.

"It is going to be okay, *mi amor*. Help is coming, yes?" Marco said.

Nikki could hear the sounds of cell phones ringing. She knew that the word was getting out, as sirens could be heard in the distance.

"Hang on, man. Ambulance is on the way. Just hang on," Derek told him.

Emergency lights flashed red from outside, their lights reflecting against the stained glass of the church. Feet were next to them—the sherriff's and paramedics'. Someone told the paramedics that there was someone in the rectory who also needed help. Nikki was being asked to move. Standing to the side in her wedding gown, Nikki leaned against the pew, feeling faint. No. She couldn't pass out. Simon needed her. Derek needed her. Marco needed her. Stay strong! As the paramedics took Simon's vitals, orders from all around were shouted out. There was crying, wailing—somewhere. A little child's cry. Violet. Where was she?

"Violet!" Marco said.

Nikki frantically searched the area to find the cries. She spotted Alyssa up near the front of the church, her face drained of color. "She's with Alyssa. I see them." Nikki ran down the aisle.

"Nikki!" Derek yelled.

She kept running, the long dress and high heels tripping her. She yanked up the dress above her ankles and kicked off the heels. Reaching Alyssa, Violet, and Petie, she said, "You have to get out of here. Take the children and go to my house. Get them out of here. Okay?"

Alyssa nodded. "Is he . . ."

"He'll be fine. He will, but you have to get the kids away from here. Jonah!" Nikki yelled.

He peered over the rectory wall and spotted them. He immediately sprinted down the back steps. Breathing hard, he took Petie into his arms.

"They need to get out of here," Nikki said.

"I agree. Come on. I'll have one of the deputies take you home. You okay, babe?" he asked.

Alyssa nodded. "I think so."

"I need you to be okay for the kids. You gotta be strong here," he said.

"I am. I'm okay. I think we should go," Alyssa replied.

"Stay here," Jonah ordered Nikki. "You're okay?" She nodded. "Good thinking."

"The cellist?" Nikki asked.

"She's okay. He knocked her out cold. Got a good bump on the back of her head, but it looks as though she'll be all right. Paramedic is with her now."

"Thank God." Nikki could feel cold seeping into her bones as another drizzle misted outside through the air. She began to shiver but more so from shock than a chill.

Jonah held Petie in one arm, his other protectively around Alyssa and Violet. Marco gave Violet a kiss good-bye. Jonah assured him that she would be fine as he escorted them outside of the church.

The paramedics loaded Simon onto a stretcher. Marco was riding to the hospital in the ambulance with him. Derek spotted Nikki down at the front of the church and went to her. He took his coat off and wrapped it around her. He pulled her in close and kissed her shoulder. "He's talking." He let out a small chuckle. "And he's talking about Prada, so my guess is he's going to be just fine." He paused, his face pale. He shook his head, and in a stutter the words came out. "Oh-my-God. It could . . . it-could-have been you." Tears filled his eyes. Nikki was not used to seeing Derek emotional, but the realization of what could have been, as well as what was, was tearing him apart. "My brother . . . and that could have been you, and it might not have been only a graze to the arm. Nikki . . ."

"It wasn't me, and I'm fine. It is Simon, though. We need to go to the hospital."

"I know."

Jonah had come back inside the church and was standing in the exact spot where Simon had gone down. He faced the rectory and looked up. "Whoever it was was no sharpshooter. From where I'm at, it looks to me to be a clean shot."

Derek stood next to Nikki, his arm around her. All of the guests were being ushered outside of the church by deputies and sectioned off into smaller groups where they were awaiting questioning by the police. Nikki was sure they were none too pleased at having to wait around for an interrogation. These were folks who, at this moment, expected to be at the Malveaux wedding reception, clinking their spoons against their wineglasses and encouraging the newly wed couple to kiss and express their love for one another.

"Do you think that whoever did this was only trying to put a scare into my brother?"

Jonah turned around and faced them. "I don't think the target was your brother."

Derek looked at Nikki. "You think . . ."

Jonah nodded. "I found something up in the rectory." Jonah took the handkerchief from his suit pocket and pulled something from another pocket. He shook it out. It was a wrinkled piece of paper. Newspaper. He showed it to them. It was their engagement photo that had run in the paper weeks before. And on the photo Nikki's face was crossed out in red ink.

"Oh my God. What? Why would someone one want to kill me?" she asked.

Jonah raised his eyebrows. "You're seriously asking that question? Let's face it, Girl Friday. It's not like you haven't made a few enemies in your days here amongst the vines."

Derek pulled her in closer. "We should tell him."

"Tell me what?" Jonah asked.

Nikki listened while Derek explained about the notes and photos.

"I see." He clucked his tongue. "I'm going to want those," Jonah said.

"I threw the first one in the garbage disposal," Nikki replied. She'd meant to dig them out the other night after the dinner with Derek's friends but had gotten distracted by the various personalities and what appeared to be some issues. She knew Derek had taken the trash out the next day because it had been trash day. Damn it. How had she overlooked that?

"I actually threw the one I got in the Dumpster behind my office."

Jonah shook his head. "Guys!"

"Who knew someone was planning this? I mean, okay, so someone was trying to kind of weird us out obviously, and neither one of us was aware that the other one was receiving this stuff, but I would have never expected this." Nikki was trying hard to keep herself together.

"Whoever did this has an agenda. Your photo wasn't the only thing I found up in the rectory."

"What else did you find?" Derek asked.

Jonah took out another photo. This one was a picture of Kenny. The images behind him were blurred. It was hard to decipher what was in the background. However the most disturbing aspect to the photo was that, like in the picture with Nikki, Kenny's face was also marked out with red ink.

"Kenny?" Nikki asked.

"What the hell?" Derek asked.

"Isn't he one of the guys who was at your rehearsal dinner last night?" Jonah asked. "Kind of the clown of the party, right?"

"That's him, and he was why I was late to the church," Derek said.

"What do you mean?" Jonah asked.

"The guys, my friends, we all thought it would be great to ride over in the limo together, have a toast. But we couldn't find Kenny. We all figured he probably went out last night after the dinner because he'd mentioned to one of the guys that he might."

"Who was that?" Jonah asked.

"Tristan. Kenny told him that he'd heard about this new hot spot over in Sonoma Square that he wanted to check out. We kind of figured that he got wasted and was still sleeping it off somewhere. I was pretty pissed off when we couldn't find him," Derek said.

"If this picture tells us a story at all, it might be to say that maybe he isn't sleeping somewhere. I have a feeling your friend could be in serious danger."

Twelve

GUILT! Oh God, so guilty feeling! Nikki dragged herself out of bed feeling like she had a weight tied around her middle and two more balanced on her shoulders.

The dream stayed with her as she walked into the kitchen to pour herself a cup of coffee. Derek was out for a morning walk with Ollie. She'd remembered him whispering in her ear about an hour or so ago. She'd tried to get up then, but he'd insisted she get some more rest. She hadn't been able to fall asleep the night before, not with everything that had happened. Derek had found some sleeping pills, and she'd taken one and finally fallen asleep in his arms. He'd been so good to her last night, reassuring her that everything was going to be okay and that they would be getting married as soon as this mess was sorted out.

She hoped he was right. *But after this morning's dream . . .* After Derek had left with Ollie and she'd fallen back asleep, she found herself dreaming of another man's arms around her. Another man in her bed. Another man waiting for her at the front of the church. Andrés. The dream had been vivid, real. She could almost smell his musky, vanilla-scented cologne when he kissed her after they were pronounced man and wife. And then an image of Simon was what had jolted her awake—Simon dripping in blood and dying in front of her. She shook as if a frozen chill had slammed through her body. What in the hell did all of that mean? She'd reached for the phone and called the hospital to learn from the nurse that Simon was asleep and had had a good night. Relieved to hear that news, she'd rolled out of bed, but the guilt remained like a thick fog.

She stirred her coffee and took a long look out the kitchen window at the vines growing along the hillside adjacent to the house, their twisted old branches intertwining together. Golden bulbs of Chardonnay grapes on the ends of leafy greens were ripening. A morning ray of sun lit up a patch of dew-soaked soil. Ripples on the clear pond spread out as the ducks maneuvered their way through the water. A mother duck and her chicks slept against the grassy bank. There weren't many sights more beautiful than the one out of their kitchen window. But no matter how hard she tried to focus on the beauty outside and the hot brew in her hands, she could not forget the painfully realistic dream. And then there was yesterday that she'd also like to forget—press rewind and start over, please. Fat chance she'd forget any of it. Her wedding day had wound up a disaster. So she stepped outside for a breath of fresh air and hoped she'd see Derek and Ollie heading her way. Nope. She sat down on the porch swing, sipping her coffee.

Doing so did not elicit the calming effect she'd hoped for. In fact, just the opposite. She found herself becoming increasingly pissed off. How dare someone try to scare her and Derek. How dare they ruin the wedding, and most of all, how dare they hurt her best friend! And how dare she dream about anyone but Derek! Damn her! Yeah, she was good and pissed off now. She couldn't necessarily control her dreams, but she could find out who was causing all of this upheaval and kick some ass. Figuratively speaking, anyway. But it was how she felt. She wanted whoever it was to be locked up for a long, long time—preferably for life.

She planned to go over to the hospital as soon as she got ready. Derek would want to go, too.

Marco had Violet now, and Alyssa and Petie had gone home with Jonah after he'd detailed his report the night before. Jonah said that he'd also be by in the morning, and Nikki knew he'd have plenty of questions. In retrospect, she'd known better than to throw away the newspaper clipping and photo she'd received, but at the time she hardly thought it would lead to an attempt on her life.

And what about Kenny? Had he come back to the inn or was he still MIA? And if he was, what did that mean, if anything at all?

Nikki spotted the newspaper on the porch and picked it up. Maybe reading about others' news would get her mind off of her own sorrows. And it worked, sort of, until she turned to the local page. There was Derek. There she was. It was their engagement photo. And the caption read, "The Wedding that Wasn't. Tragedy for Napa Valley's Malveaux Family." What the hell? But it got worse when

she spotted who had written the column—Renee Rothschild! Whoa . . . hold your horses! Nikki scanned the
article and, upon doing so, decided that either someone
who'd attended "The Wedding that Wasn't" had given
Renee the details of what had happened or somehow she
had sneaked into the church herself. She certainly had
not been invited. Who had taken those photos?

For starters, Renee had an exact description of Nikki's dress and the flowers—all of it was written about in
her gossipy, icky piece. Nikki crumpled up the paper but
then caved in and unfolded it to reread it.

The Wedding that Wasn't

What was supposed to be the best day of their
lives and the wedding of all weddings in Napa
Valley yesterday turned suddenly tragic for Derek
Malveaux and Nikki Sands.

The beautifully decorated St. Luke's Church
held nearly four hundred of the couple's guests.
The bride wore Badgley Mischka and, with her
new pixie-cut, platinum blond hairdo, looked
stunning in the crystal-laden silk sheath that
certainly must have cost a pretty penny. But, after
all, she was marrying one of Napa Valley's golden
boys, for years a seriously sought after bachelor
amongst the vines. But it may be that the catch
amidst men could be single soon after yesterday's
ordeal—what with the black cloud of death lurking
around Nikki Sands.

As the bride made her way down the aisle, a
gunshot rang out. The guests, first shocked and

then frightened, took cover as Detective Jonah Robinson of the Sonoma County sherriff's department quickly took charge of the situation and went running up the back stairs of the rectory. There he found the cellist had been knocked out and the gunman had gotten away. The groom's brother Simon Malveaux was hit in the arm and suffered injuries. He was taken to Valley of Hope where he was treated and is in good condition.

With a gunman on the loose, and the should-be honeymooners having to regroup, this reporter has to wonder if it's in the cards for a Malveaux/Sands wedding to actually take place. One guest speaking anonymously said, "I don't think I'd tempt fate again. Not after what happened today. Maybe they just weren't meant to be married."

Nikki crumpled the paper up even harder this time and let out a loud gasp. "Of all the gall!" Who would write something so cruel? And what anonymous guest used that damn word "fate"? Nikki had to find out.

She went back inside and hurriedly got dressed. She was on a mission to find Renee Rothschild. As far as she was concerned, not only did that woman owe her an apology, but she also had some explaining to do.

Thirteen

NIKKI didn't really think about how she was going to find Renee. She wouldn't be in her office in San Francisco today. It was Sunday, and damn it, Nikki should've been on the Malveaux jet at that moment with her husband on their way to Italy!

What was she thinking trying to find this woman? But Renee had seriously gotten under her skin. What she'd written was trashy and wrong. It was one thing to report what had happened. Nikki had expected that. The facts were the facts—a gunman did injure Simon and their wedding *had* been ruined. But to write such conjecture and b.s. about a possible breakup between her and Derek. And Nikki planned on getting the name of the *anonymous* guest. She had to know who had used the word that seemed to be haunting her. And when had Renee even interviewed anyone from the wedding? Again, the thought that Renee could have actually attended entered

Nikki's mind. There had been a sea of people in the church. There was no way she would have noticed Renee as she walked down the aisle. She certainly would have been the last person she'd expect to see at her wedding. Nikki tightened her grip on the steering wheel. Likely Renee had been a wedding crasher. Of all the nerve!

She thought about seeing Renee with Andrés just two days ago when she'd been out with Ollie, and she had a hunch that Renee hadn't left Napa to go back to the city at all. If Nikki was right, she knew exactly where to find her.

Driving up the winding hill to Andrés' driveway, Nikki spotted the blue Beemer. Her hunch had been correct: Renee Rothschild had seduced her way right into Andrés' life, and from the looks of it, his bed as well.

Nikki's hands were shaking when she knocked on Andrés' front door. How weird it was to be standing here like this when only a little more than a year before she would have just walked right on in? She heard laughter coming from inside. This was insanely stupid. She needed to get her bearings and think logically. Irrationality was going to get her nowhere, and the sounds of Renee and Andrés laughing together inside turned her stomach. Nikki was heading back to her car when the front door opened and out came a giggling Andrés and Renee. Renee wearing one of Andrés' shirts over a pair of his sweat pants—sweats that Nikki had once worn.

"Nikki?" Andrés said.

She turned back around. "Hi," she replied, chagrined.

He looked at her oddly. "Why . . . why are you here? What about, uh, how was your wedding?"

She stood there staring at him and then went back to

her car and grabbed the crumpled up newspaper from the front seat and handed it to him. Renee's eyes popped.

"What is this? I don't understand," he said.

"Read it." Nikki smiled at Renee. "I have to wonder when you found time to write this. It looks as if you've been busy."

Renee looked down and then back at Nikki. "Look, I was only doing my job. That's all. No harm, no foul. I was only reporting the news."

Andrés finished reading and took a hard look at Renee as though he was seeing her for the first time. "You wrote this?"

"I did, but like I just explained to Nikki, I was only doing my job."

"But this is, this is . . ."

"Mean," Nikki interrupted. "It's callous, and it's mean. Yesterday I was supposed to marry Derek and something terrible happened. My friend, my future brother-in-law, was hurt and could have been killed, and you treat it like it's a *National Enquirer* story. And what was that all about saying that Derek could be back on the market? Please. You wish."

"Oh, come on, Nikki. I'm obviously over Derek." She tugged at the bottom hem of Andrés' shirt.

"Huh. In my book there is a difference between reporting the facts and making up salacious scandals, which is exactly what you did."

"Please. That's what readers expect from my column."

"So you'll write this crap at the expense of others? About people you know? It's hurtful, Renee."

Renee shrugged. "It isn't exactly as if we're best pals, Nik. Seems to me you kinda stole my man."

Nikki took a step back as if she'd been struck. "What?"

"Yeah, and then you left this poor guy here hanging in the lurch. Trust me, I know all about it." She smiled at Andrés. "Sorry, my Latin lover, but as good as you are in the sack, and, well, let's just say it was *really* good." She gave Nikki a look full of devious joy. "I have heard more about this woman in the last two days than I ever cared to know."

"What?" Nikki and Andrés shouted simultaneously.

Renee glared at Nikki. "Oh, yeah, girlfriend, seems you have some pheromones that men don't easily get over. I don't know what your secret is, but first Derek, then this guy."

"I think you should go," Andrés said.

Renee looked at him, surprise clouding her face. "Fine. If that's the way you feel. I should have known that as soon as Blondie showed up it'd be all over. I'll have my office call you then, and we can set up a time next week to work on the project."

"I am not working with you," he said.

"Yes, you are. You signed a contract. And please remember to keep the blabbering about Blondie here down to a minimum when we meet up again. I am not a good shoulder to cry on. We can get it on any time of the day, but I am not here to mend any hearts. I have to grab my things."

Nikki and Andrés didn't look at each other when Renee dashed back into the house. Nikki had no clue what to say, and she got the feeling that Andrés didn't either.

A minute later, out came Renee. "Thanks for the memories." She kissed Andrés on the cheek. He wiped it away. "See you soon."

"Wait a minute," Nikki said. "You owe me. You can't just leave. I think you owe me an apology. And you need to tell me who your source is. Who did you interview for this story?"

Renee laughed. "Sure."

"You know I need to know who the anonymous guest was that made the comment about our wedding not happening having something to do with fate. It has to do with the investigation." Not usually at a loss for words, Nikki was finding it difficult to express herself at all at that moment. There was so much more she wanted and needed to say to Renee. She needed information from her. "If you don't give me the information, I'll have you fired." Even as the words came out of her mouth, she realized how ridiculous they sounded. Sure—have Renee fired from the company her father happened to own.

"Oh, please, Nikki. Even you can't be that naïve. I'm a reporter and a publisher. I don't give up my sources." She held her arm out straight. "And your threats have me shaking." She tossed back her hair.

"Renee! That's just wrong. I'm going to sue you for slander, or libel, or something!"

Renee started her car, put down the convertible top, and laughed. "Go for it!" She peeled out and drove down the drive.

Andrés and Nikki stood there, not knowing what to

say or do. Nikki finally turned to him, and before she could stop herself, she asked, "What did she mean that she'd heard more than enough about me?"

Without looking at her he let out a long sigh and replied, "I'm still in love with you."

"Please take that back," Nikki whispered, unable to look at Andrés. "Please don't mean that."

"I'm sorry."

Nikki closed her eyes and shook her head. "I am getting married. I am going to marry Derek. I can't talk to you about this. You moved on. You said so. You don't mean that."

He took a step toward her. "I do mean it, and I am sorry. I do not want to be a problem for you. Tell me you don't have any feelings for me at all anymore, and I will go back to Spain and you will marry Derek."

Tears in her eyes, she shook a finger at him. Feeling her face contort into confusion and anger, she said, "I am going to marry Derek and you should go back to Spain."

"So you have no feelings left for me? None?" His dark eyes sparkled in the sunlight. He lifted his chin slightly. Standing there in his jeans and white T-shirt, the newspaper in his hand, tendrils of his dark hair that had grown longer since he'd left for Spain fell into his eyes as he studied her, made him seem poetic and, in a way, tragic. It was like he could see right through her.

"That is a stupid question! Of course I care about you. We were friends. We are friends! We, well that is it. We're friends." She thought about the dream she'd had that morning. And she couldn't look at him.

He nodded. "Okay. Friends. We are friends then."

"I have to go." She got into her car, and Andrés walked over to her as she started it. She rolled down the window.

"Maybe Renee got one thing right in her article. Is it possible that this is a sign? That you and Derek are not meant to be married," he said.

"Ugh," she moaned, and rolled up her window. She drove away, but couldn't help looking in her rearview mirror—Andrés standing there, arms crossed in front of him and an amused smile on his face.

Fourteen

"WHAT'S going on?" Nikki asked the guard at the front gate of Malveaux Estate. A sign on the gate read that they were closed for the day.

The guard—a beefy, but nice enough guy—shrugged. "Don't know. But must be bad. Sherriff pulled in thirty or so minutes ago, and so did that detective along with an ambulance and, a few minutes ago, another van. Driver handed me a badge. It said . . ."

"I know what it said." Nikki pressed her clicker and went into the gate, leaving the guard behind.

She drove up the hill past their house, up toward the winery. She didn't see any emergency vehicles yet.

Parked next to the warehouse that held the steel wine vats, she spotted Jonah's sedan, three sheriffs' cars, and an ambulance. Then there was the van she shouldn't have been able to recognize so easily but did—the coroner. She jumped out of her car and sprinted over to where she spotted Jonah and some other officers talking outside the warehouse entrance. Out of breath, she said, "What's going on? Where's Derek?"

"Derek!" Jonah yelled. "I found her!"

"Found her? Found me? What?"

Derek came running out of the warehouse. He wrapped his arms around her and held her tight. She could feel his heart pounding hard against his chest. "Where have you been? Where the hell have you been!"

"I-I-I . . ." Yeah right—tell him where she was? Sure that would go over real well. "What is going on here? What is this all about?"

He pulled away from her. "Kenny." He choked back emotion. "I found him in one of the tanks. He went into one of the gassed tanks and . . ."

"Oh my God." Nikki brought a hand up to her mouth. She knew exactly what that meant. A few of the tanks hadn't been filled yet with wine. And the gasses from fermentation inside the empty tanks were extremely lethal. Without wearing the proper equipment someone would die of asphyxiation in only a few breaths. "Why would he do that? Why go into one of the empty tanks?" she asked.

Jonah sighed. "We're looking at all angles. Could have been suicide, but there's no note, and he'd have to have been aware of the fact that going inside the tank would kill him. It could have been accidental—curiosity. Derek mentioned he was interested in how the wine was made when you all took a tour the other day around here, and that he was especially interested in the tanks. Made a comment about wanting to try the wine straight out of it."

She nodded. "I remember. He *was* interested and *did*

make that comment. I just can't believe this. It's crazy. I don't know what to say. I mean he actually climbed down into it. I don't get it. I really don't understand."

"Like I said, we are looking at all possibilities, Nikki, including murder."

Nikki nodded. "Right."

"We need to check this area out completely," Jonah said. "I'd also like to come down to the house when we're finished and talk to you both about last night. If we are looking at murder, then my guess is this is all connected, considering the photos we found in the church. We will have to put police tape up around the perimeter. We can't have anyone in and out of here until we sweep the area."

"Of course. I've already radioed to the front gate guard that we are closed today."

"Good. So, why don't the two of you head on down, try to relax, and I'll be by in a bit."

"My car is right over there," Nikki said.

"Let's just walk down, honey. I could use it. I want to think, breathe. I don't know. We can come back up in a bit and get your car."

"Sure. No problem," she replied.

Derek took her hand in his, and they started down the path to their house. "This is too much. I don't know what to think. First the threats, then Simon, and now this? You know it could be something more than just Kenny's curiosity that did him in. I mean we could be looking at someone who is out to kill. Nik, I know we are. I think there is a psychopath on the loose. Look at yesterday. I think we need to get you out of here. I think you need to go and visit your aunt. Go to Italy until this guy is caught."

Nikki stopped walking. "No! What are you saying? No way. First of all, we don't know who fired off that gun yesterday. We don't know for sure if it was really meant for me. I am sure Simon has made an enemy or two in his day. And the weird threats or whatever you'd call them that we've been getting—and this today, with Kenny—we really can't say for sure that it's all connected. I'm not going anywhere. For one thing, if these things are even connected, how do we know that whoever is behind this will even be caught? I can't believe you would want to send me away."

"I don't. I know you're right, but we have to assume there is a killer who wanted you dead and who has now killed Kenny." He shook his head. "I was so worried about you. I took Ollie out for the walk, cruised through the winery and warehouses, and that's when I saw that the one tank had been opened. I quickly grabbed a mask to see what was going on because Manuel was out on the back forty managing the cutting of the new vines. You weren't there, but I thought maybe you'd gone to see Simon. So, I went back up to the tank and that's when I found Kenny. I called Jonah, and then I called Simon to see if you were with him. He said that he hadn't heard from you. He was pretty groggy, but Marco was with him, and he said that he hadn't heard from you either. I called you again and no answer."

"I left my cell in the car. I'm sorry."

He hugged her again. "I know, but damn it, when I couldn't find you after everything . . . and then finding Kenny, my mind ran rampant with every thought possible. I was scared. I was out of my mind scared."

She looked up into his green eyes and kissed him.

Their kiss grew intense and heated. Passionate. When they pulled away, he stroked her cheek. "I don't ever want to lose you."

"You're not going to ever lose me," she said.

They walked down to the house. Derek let go of her hand to open the front door. Ollie bounded toward her. "Hi, you. I had you worried too, huh?" She glanced back at Derek.

"Looks like it. We were all wondering where you'd gone off to." He shut the door behind him. "So, where did you go, babe? Where were you?"

Fifteen

"YOU were where? Why in the hell were you at Andrés' place?" Derek was pacing the hardwood floors in the family room. Ollie crouched down by the couch, keeping a watchful eye on him.

She shook her head. "Just sit down, please, and hear me out. It's not anything like what you think," Nikki replied.

"Really? And what might I be thinking? Why would I be thinking anything? What? Just because the guy you used to be with, who was madly in love with you, who invited you to come live with him in Spain, who wanted you to marry him, is back in Napa and you were at his house this morning? What would I be thinking, Nik?"

"Oh, come on! Renee Rothschild was with him."

Derek stared hard at her. "What?"

"I take it that you didn't see the morning's newspaper."

"No."

"Okay, you may want to take a look at the article your ex-girlfriend—who, might I remind you, you almost took with you to Australia—wrote, a not so nice article about our wedding debacle. Even going so far as to suggest a breakup between us." Nikki was now pacing the floor. She hated this. They sounded so childish, immature, stupid. This was no way for either of them to be acting. Their emotions had gotten the best of them.

He shut his mouth tight for a few seconds, as if looking for the right words. "I'm confused."

"Let me clear it up for you."

Nikki explained to him about running into Andrés and Renee and how when she read the article that morning that she had become inflamed and had a hunch she'd find Renee over at Andrés' place, where she intended to find out who the anonymous guest was that used the word "fate." And to drag an apology out of that woman.

"You've known for three days that Andrés has been back in town?"

Nikki tossed her arms up. "Are you serious right now? Out of everything I just told you, that's your concern."

"Shouldn't it be?"

"Um . . . No! I didn't tell you because it was really low on my radar. You and I were supposed to be getting married yesterday, and running into Andrés and Renee didn't even rank."

Derek stopped pacing. "Oh, jeez. I don't know . . . I'm sorry, baby. I am so stupid. I don't know what's got into me. I know you love me. I love you. I lost it. Stupid. Jealousy is stupid and should not be a factor here. There is so much more to worry about."

Nikki nodded. "Yes, there is. Your brother and now Kenny."

She walked over and wrapped her arms around him. "You are the one for me. Okay? I made that clear when I went with you to Australia. At least I thought I did. I only went to Andrés' place to confront Renee."

"I know. I need to talk with her. She needs to write a retraction or something."

"No. What she needs to do is tell us who she interviewed and if she was in the church herself yesterday. I don't trust her at all."

"You're right. I need to get a hold of everyone. Jonah wants the guests who were here to stay until he can question them, and I should be the one to go and tell our friends."

She nodded. "Do you want me to go up to the hotel with you?" she asked.

"No. Stay here. I'll be back soon. I know Jonah will be down in a bit."

"Okay."

He started for the door and stopped. "You know what, actually? Why don't you come with me? Maybe this is something we should do together. I could use your support."

"Sure, honey. I'm here for you."

They headed out the door. Nikki couldn't help wondering if Derek's change of mind was really about needing her support or wanting to keep her close to him because someone appeared to want her dead.

Sixteen

EVERYONE except Lily was lounging around the pool, but the usual energy poolside wasn't there today. The news she and Derek were about to deliver was only going to add to that.

Savannah, her nose buried in a magazine with a half-empty bottle of champagne at her side, looked up first. Nikki thought it an odd choice to be drinking champagne, when as far as she was concerned there was nothing to be celebrating. Then again all Savannah was aware of thus far was that no wedding had taken place. Maybe she was actually celebrating that fact. Tristan was on the opposite end of the pool, flanked by Zach on one side and Jackson on the other.

"Oh, hello," Savannah said.

Nikki nodded. "Good morning."

Derek led her by the hand and they sat down on a free

lounge chair. "We have something to tell everyone. Is Lily around?" he asked.

"No," Jackson replied. "She said that she was going into town to the farmers' market. How's your brother?"

"He's doing good. I spoke with him this morning, and he's going to be released from the hospital shortly. Marco will be bringing him home. He'll have quite a bit of physical therapy with the shoulder, but the good news is he's going to be fine."

"That's wonderful," Zach said and took a sip from his iced tea. "But why are you all so grim then? We were hoping you'd be by to tell us when the new wedding will happen."

Derek and Nikki looked at each other. "We haven't talked about a new date yet," Derek said.

"Oh. Well you are getting married, aren't you?" Savannah asked with obvious feigned concern.

"Of course we are," Derek replied. "But something has come up and it concerns everyone here."

"What are you talking about?" Tristan took a swig from a beer bottle.

"This isn't easy, gang, but you know how we all assumed that Kenny hadn't shown up for the wedding because he was out partying?"

"Yeah. Must be some party because we still haven't seen hide nor hair of him," Jackson mused.

"Doesn't that make you all wonder?" Nikki asked. Sure she knew Kenny was dead, but the fact that none of his friends appeared remotely concerned that this man hadn't shown up in over twenty-four hours bothered her.

Jackson shrugged. "That's Kenny," Zach said. "He's known for choosing the party over anything else."

•

"He didn't this time," Derek cut in.

"Jeez, you two. What gives? Knock off the mystery crap and tell us what is going on," Tristan insisted.

"Kenny is dead," Derek blurted out.

Nikki studied each one of his friend's faces for reaction. Savannah's jaw dropped. Zach looked puzzled. Jackson and Tristan both remained expressionless. Odd.

It was Jackson who spoke first. "What do you mean? What in the world are you talking about? Dead? No. He's not dead."

Nikki couldn't help notice Savannah dot her eyes underneath her sunglasses. Was she crying? "How? How did he die?" she choked.

"He got into one of the wine tanks and was asphyxiated."

"I don't believe this," Zach said.

"I know," Derek said. "After yesterday, I needed to clear my head with a morning walk and then get about my usual routine. I spotted one of the wine tank doors cracked open. That's not normal. My guys who clean those tanks would never leave the door open. To do so in the first place you have to go in there with the proper equipment. The gasses inside the tank will kill someone in minutes. When I checked it out, I found Kenny."

Savannah brought a hand up to her mouth. Her tears were obvious now. Nikki couldn't help but wonder at her deeply emotional response. Savannah hadn't struck her as the sensitive sort. Sure it was horrible, and being upset was a natural reaction, but for Savannah to be this upset about one of her husband's college buddies didn't quite add up. It led Nikki to believe what she'd already suspected—that Savannah and Kenny's friendship had been something more. Her response and actions to Kenny's arrival the other night would be right on par with the way she was reacting now to his death, if indeed there had been something clandestine going on between the two of them. Her thoughts on this made Nikki take another look at Tristan. Hard to tell what he was thinking with his sunglasses covering his eyes. Nikki knew that much could be told by the look in someone's eye, and she had to wonder if she would have found a sadness like the one in Zach's eyes or the shock that Jackson's seemed to convey. What if Tristan's had more of a gleam? Could he have been on to—something going on between his wife and old pal?

"What do the police think?" Savannah sobbed.

"They aren't saying a whole lot right now," Derek replied.

Nikki cleared her throat. She knew she shouldn't go where she was about to go because Derek was probably going to give her the evil eye, but what the hell. Reactions were what she was looking for, because if Kenny had been murdered, the murderer could be right there seated around the pool. "The detective in charge did mention that it could be an accident, possible suicide . . ." She paused and took a deep breath. "And they have not ruled out murder."

"Nikki," Derek said warningly.

She shrugged. "I'm just relaying what's going on. I think it's only fair that everyone is fully aware of the situation. Besides, Detective Robinson suggested that everyone who was here for the wedding stay put for a couple of days until he has a chance to question them."

Derek eyed her. She knew she was blowing smoke.

Jonah hadn't said anything of the sort to her, and as far as she knew, he hadn't to Derek either. But what the heck? She had a feeling, and many times her feelings had been dead-on. If Nikki was a gambling gal she'd place a bet that Kenny had been murdered. A few things had her perplexed though. The first was whether someone had lured Kenny into that tank or dragged him there? An autopsy and toxicology report might determine that. The second question had to do with the shooter at the church—if Kenny had been murdered, were the shooter and the murderer the same person? And the third and final question was the most troubling. The ominous notes and photos she and Derek had received, followed by the horrible events that had taken place at their wedding, led to a disturbing thought: was someone out to get the bride and the groom?

Seventeen

"WHAT was that all about?" Derek asked Nikki on their way back down to the house.

"What was what all about?" Nikki asked innocently, knowing perfectly well what he was getting at.

He stopped, dropped her hand, and looked at her. "I know you. I know what's going on in your head, and you know exactly what I'm talking about. Bringing up the idea that Kenny might have been murdered around my friends was totally out of line, and you know it was. Jonah said nothing about keeping those people around. You're going straight into Nancy Drew mode, and this time I am going to insist—no, demand—that you knock it off. You're not a detective. You are not a police officer. Enough is enough."

She stared at him for a good long second or two, trying to wrap her brain around what he'd just said to her.

"Did you just tell me that you are *demanding* I do or not do something?"

"Yes. I believe that I am. No I don't *believe* that I am. I am."

Nikki didn't quite know how to respond to his "demands." And what came out of her mouth next was something that she would quickly regret. "You know, Derek, we aren't married yet."

It was his turn to stare at her. "No, we're not. I'm not sure what you even mean by that."

She sighed. Now was the time to stop while she was still sort of ahead. She was smart enough to know better. "What I mean is that . . ." Oh crap, what did she mean by that exactly? "What I mean is that married or not, I don't think people who love each other make demands on one another."

"Nikki, you are being totally ridiculous here. You know that I love you more than anything in the world, and for you to imply that I don't is stupid. I don't want you getting involved in any of this for your own good. How many times now has it been that you've almost been hurt, or even killed, by sticking your nose into business that you have no business sticking it into?"

She wasn't going to give up that easily. "I don't think I have no business in this, and frankly you should be sticking your nose into this as well. Let's look at the facts here. Both of us have been receiving notes and photos with 'fate' written on them leading all the way up to our wedding day. Then Simon is shot on our wedding day with a bullet likely meant for me. Now Kenny is found dead and you have some rather interesting friends hanging around here. Not to mention there are a handful of enemies in the vicinity who might want to cause us harm. Nothing like murder and mayhem hanging over us to distract from the bliss we should certainly be experiencing right about now. You know what? If you're such a big fan of us making demands on each other, then I have a demand for you. You demand that I keep my nose out of this? Well, I demand that you get your nose into this. Deep in it. Immediately. How do you like that? Does that feel good? Because here is the deal, Derek. I don't do demands—married or not. I will not do demands. I appreciate that you're worried about me, I do. But watch your mouth. We are partners, not each other's keepers. We need each other. I say we join forces and find out why someone out there wants to keep us apart and ruin our future. Because if I had to make a guess about any of this, I would guess that is exactly what someone is after."

Derek didn't respond right away, and Nikki was preparing herself for an onslaught of anger and frustration. To her surprise, though, he took her hand and said, "I'm sorry. I really am. I didn't mean to sound like I did. Sometimes I think I must be out of my mind to love you, because you are the most stubborn woman I have ever known. But damn it, Nancy Drew, I am hooked. And you're right. About everything. I'm in. Where do we start?"

Eighteen

BEFORE they could jump into figuring out the mystery behind all that had happened in the past couple of days at the vineyard, Nikki and Derek spotted Marco's Prius coming up the road. After adding Violet to their family, Simon and Marco had decided that going green was the responsible parental thing to do. It helped that the two of them had studied with Alan Sansi (also known as the popular Guru Sansibaba). Alan had become a good friend of Nikki and Derek's as well, and his latest book, *On Parenting Responsibly in an Age of Irresponsibility* had hit the bestseller list and Alan had wound up on *Oprah*.

"Looks like our patient has arrived," Derek said. "I think we should go and see if they need some help."

"I agree, but there is a problem," Nikki replied.

"What's that?"

"Patrice and her new husband." In all of the commotion

and confusion, Nikki hadn't had a chance to update Derek on his stepmother's status on the vineyard and that she was still in the mansion on the hill. She was sure that Marco was sooner rather than later going to come unglued about it, as Simon had indicated to her at the rehearsal. "We need to do something about getting her out of here."

Derek nodded. "Let me handle it."

Nikki held up her hands. "I have no problem with that."

They drove up the hill to the main house. Simon was being helped out of the car by Marco. Violet was in the back in her car seat, giggling her precious two-year-old giggle. Nikki couldn't help but smile. "Hey," she said. "Can we help?"

Marco glanced over. "Want to get the baby?" he asked.

"You don't have to ask me twice," she said but first gave Simon a kiss on the cheek. "How's it going?"

He rolled his eyes at her. "How do you think it's going, sister? Some maniac tried to take my arm off. I'll never look good in a tank top again. And what's going to happen to this body? I have to take time off from my workout. My tummy is going to go to pot."

"I think that's probably the last thing you should worry your mind over, *mi amor*," Marco said. "You are gorgeous no matter what."

"He's right," Nikki said.

"Probably," Simon replied.

Derek opened up Violet's door and unfastened her car seat. He winked at Nikki. "Beat you to it." He kissed Violet and tickled her. More laughter.

"What can we do for you, Si?" Nikki asked.

He looked at her with sad puppy dog eyes. "Oh, nothing, doll. You've already been through so much. Really, you don't need to bother."

"What do you need?" she insisted.

He sighed heavily. "Okay, then, if you're going to badger me, I need all organic fruits and veggies. We're going to need sushi grade ahi for this evening. You do such a good job with that black sesame seed recipe. You know the one where you sear the fish and then drizzle that poblano sauce over it."

Nikki smiled. "Excuse me, but I didn't know that I would be fixing dinner."

Simon pouted.

"Of course I'll fix you dinner. On one condition. You have to come down to the ranch house. I won't make dinner for Patrice."

"Did I hear someone call my name?" Patrice was walking toward them, flanked by a golden-tanned, muscle man with eyes the color of a Mediterranean sea. His facial features were large—almost overexaggerated. He had a crop of thick curly dark hair. He wasn't attractive except that his eyes were startling—the color was so intense and beautiful that it was hard not to stare. Plus, his muscles were obviously steroid grade. He was quite a sight.

"Hello, mother," Simon said as she ran up and air kissed each side of his cheek.

"Oh, darling. Adonis and I have been so worried about you."

Adonis. Of course. Perfect. And Greek. *The notes.*

"If you were so *worried*, Mother Dear, then why didn't you come to the hospital?" Simon asked.

Good. Maybe the fact that his mother didn't take any time out of her evening last night to go and see her only son who had been shot in the shoulder would be enough to convince him to help chase her off the Malveaux property. Violet reached out for her grandmother from Derek's arms.

"Sweet babe, come to Pit Pat." She glanced at everyone. "It sounds so much better than grandma."

Nikki was thinking she might just vomit right there on the spot.

Derek held tighter onto Violet. "I'll take her into the house, and then you and I need to discuss a few things, Patrice."

Patrice took a step back and her eyes widened. Adonis wrapped a massive arm around her shoulder. "Such a warm welcome from my darling stepson," Patrice trilled.

Derek didn't acknowledge the remark but started toward the front door of the mansion. Marco opened the trunk of the car and took out Simon's bag. Nikki took Simon's uninjured arm and walked with him into the house. He leaned into her and whispered, "I have a feeling this is going to be better than an episode of *The Real Housewives of New Jersey*."

"You could be right," Nikki replied.

Simon and Marco had done some updating to the mansion, which for years had remained somewhere between 1982 and 1987 in unappealing shades of green and burgundy. Simon had sunk some money into new hardwood floors, and the color scheme had been changed to earth tones and golds—a vision to reflect the vines that grew outside. The kitchen still needed some serious updating, but Nikki had the feeling that Marco and Simon had rested in a holding pattern with the assumption that eventually Mommy Dearest would return and want her abode back. Hopefully, Derek would be able to talk some sense into the old crow.

"Where would you like to rest, *mi amor*?" Marco asked.

"In the sunroom sounds nice. Can I get a glass of iced tea as well? And maybe some of those little butter cookies we have in the cookie jar?"

"Of course."

Derek handed Violet to Nikki. "Why don't you take the baby and Si into the garden room? I need to speak with Patrice alone."

"I don't think that's necessary," Patrice remarked.

"It is. And when I say alone, I mean alone." He eyed Adonis.

Adonis shrugged. "You will be fine, no? I will go in the garden room and make discussion with your son and . . ." he said with a Greek accent.

"Nikki," Nikki said. "Really that's okay. I think Simon needs his rest."

"But I would like to get to know you better. You are all my family now, too. I have a big family at home, and I miss family."

"Trust me, buddy, this is not anything like your family at home, I'm pretty sure." Nikki studied him for a moment and in a strange way felt sorry for the big lug. What kind of spell had Patrice put on him? Likely the money spell.

"Be nice," Simon said.

"Okay. Only for you, and only because you're hurt."

Nikki carried Violet as she followed Simon into the garden room. Adonis walked in behind them. Marco went to make a pitcher of iced tea, and Derek and Patrice went off into the living room to hopefully have a civilized discussion and come up with the only result that would benefit everyone—her leaving the vineyard.

Simon stretched out on the floral yellow garden sofa, and Violet immediately climbed out of Nikki's arms and went straight for her basket of toys in the corner of the room. Nikki and Adonis sat opposite one another in white wicker chairs.

She crossed her legs and clasped her hands around her knees. Smiling at Adonis, she figured small talk was the way to go. "So, Adonis, right?" He nodded. "How did you meet Patrice?"

His goofy smile spread across his face. "Amazing. I was in class and this beautiful woman comes in and takes a seat next to mine. I was so in luck. It was love at first sight."

"Really? That's amazing. A class, huh? What kind of class? Where was this?"

"In Greece, of course. We were learning of Greek mythology and the gods of fate."

Nineteen

"YOU asked me where we start with this thing," Nikki said as she and Derek arrived home.

Derek looked at her confused.

"With the gunshot and Kenny."

"Yeah. I'm sorry. I'm a little distracted. My conversation didn't go as planned with Patrice."

"Uh-oh. That doesn't sound too good."

"No. Not really. I'm going to have to call our attorneys and see what we can do."

"Well, we certainly can't all live as one big happy family. God knows we aren't the Brady Bunch."

"I know that," he said sounding irritated. "But it might be more difficult than I thought."

"Why?"

"I don't want to talk about it right now."

"Okay," Nikki replied.

Derek walked in and plopped down on the sofa. A

heavy sigh left his lips. He patted the sofa. "Come over here."

Nikki sat down next to him. He put his arm around her, and she leaned her head on his shoulder. "This all really sucks, doesn't it," she said.

"It sure does. But I think you're right. We need to take some action. I need to call the attorneys and get Patrice out of here. And we do need to figure out who has been sending those notes, taking a shot at Simon, and who killed Kenny."

"We do. Jonah just left me a message about stopping by here. He was hoping to catch us in the next hour. I sent him a text to let him know we would be around. I do need to go into town though and pick up Simon's groceries and get dinner prepped for tonight. I told him and Marco to come down around seven."

"I can run into town if you'd like," Derek said.

"No. I've got it. I know everything that we need."

"I don't think I want you going alone, babe. Not with what we know about this case. Someone seems to have a vendetta and you're on the list of this . . . what did he sign his name with?"

"Moros Apate Thanatos."

"Weird."

"It is weird. You're assuming that whoever this psycho is, is a man," Nikki said.

"I suppose I am. The guy shot from the rectory of the church. Made his way out of the church without anyone getting near him. I'm inclined to think we're dealing with a man here. To hit the cellist hard enough on the head and sprint out of here, the person had to be fairly strong and fast."

Nikki nodded. "Man? Maybe, maybe not. There are plenty of strong and fast women around. But here is something interesting. Adonis and your step-monster met at a Greek mythology class. And here's something you may not have noticed about Patrice that I have."

"What's that?"

"The woman looks like she's been to boot camp. Sure, she's what, seventy? But have you gotten a good look at that bod? She's been working out."

Derek shook his head. "Oh, come on now. You don't really think that Patrice is involved in all of this? Besides she didn't even know Kenny."

"Good point, but maybe we are dealing with two separate issues here. Or maybe Patrice and Adonis are working together and Kenny's murder—and my gut tells me it *was* murder—was committed because they wanted to throw the police off. Because, let's face it, the tie-in makes no sense." Nikki reached down and scratched behind Ollie's ears as he plopped down on the floor next to her feet.

"I don't know. Maybe. Patrice doesn't like you. That's no secret. It's no secret that I have no need for her either, but as far as a motive? I don't know."

"I'm a threat, Derek. I always have been. I'm about to be your wife, and she sees me as a threat. I'm also the reason her daughter and son are behind bars. If I'd never come here then those two may have been able to get their way, and Patrice would be running this winery. Tell me that's not a motive for murder."

"You don't think that Meredith could have been in communication with Patrice, do you?" Derek asked, referring to his ex-wife. An ex-wife who no one, not even

Simon, had known was related to Patrice. Patrice had put Meredith and her brother up for adoption, and it was years later that Patrice brought them back into her life with some wild scheme to take over the Malveaux winery and vineyard. The problem was that Meredith and her brother Cal had taken it a step too far, and Meredith had become romantically involved with the Malveaux's winemaker at the time, who eventually called it off with her. Meredith had killed him, and her brother had helped her cover it up. They then took their plans even further by plotting to kill Derek. However, by that point, Nikki had complicated things by coming into the picture. "Maybe Meredith is talking to Patrice. I guess it's an angle we can't ignore," Derek continued, sensing Nikki's glare.

"I think one of the first things we need to do is get on the Internet and find out as much as we can about the gods of fate in Greek mythology and all about the ones that this person or persons signs his or her name with, Moros Apate Thanatos. I also think we have to look at all of the other possibilities, including learning a little bit more about your friends and their recent histories." Derek raised his eyebrows. Nikki continued, "I told you that you weren't going to like some of this. But the facts are the facts. All of your pals here knew Kenny, and I have a feeling not everyone cared too much for him. Why any of them would want me dead, I'm not too sure. We know why Patrice might want me six feet under, but your college friends? That is a mystery. People change sometimes, Derek. Who knows why they do what they do. But the signature alone, the messages we've been getting, speaks of someone who has been methodically planning this out for some time. And not only that, it speaks of someone who is far more dangerous than just your average killer."

Derek laughed.

"What's funny?" she asked.

"Aren't all killers dangerous?" he asked, still laughing. "I know this isn't a joking matter, but the way that came out . . . I'm sorry, hon."

She socked him lightly on his shoulder. "I know what you mean and, yes, of course *all* killers are dangerous. However, most killers tend to kill someone close to them due to a crime of passion, an argument that makes them snap, that kind of thing."

"Okay. I think I'm seeing your point. Whoever is behind this, assuming it's one person, then they've planned it out. It wasn't a spur of the moment decision, and it sounds like a psychopath."

"Ooh, now you're cooking, and I am finding it very, very sexy."

"Really?" he said.

"Uh-huh. Really."

He looked at his watch. "What time did you say Jonah would be by?"

"In about thirty minutes. Why?" she asked.

"I was thinking that this Internet stuff could wait until after dinner tonight. It sounds like it could really take us some time."

"It does, doesn't it? But I'm still not finished filling you in on my plan," she said.

"Can't your plan wait? You can fill me in when we go into town together."

"I told you that I'd be fine alone."

"This is supposed to be our honeymoon, you know.

And if we're going to puzzle this mystery out together, then we should probably be spending quite a bit of time together."

"Good point."

"In the meantime, though," he said, "while we're waiting for Jonah, I could stand to have my batteries recharged. This investigating stuff sounds exhausting."

She shook her head. "What did you have in mind?"

"Oh, I think you know."

The doorbell rang before Nikki could take Derek up on his offer. "Looks like Jonah is early."

"Damn detective has the worst timing."

Nikki opened the door. Ollie barked and growled until he realized it was Jonah, who breezed in and sat down across from Derek. Nikki walked back into the family room. Jonah was not one for formalities.

"Well, kids, I can tell you for certain that your friend Kenny was murdered. Coroner says he was hit with a blunt object and then dragged into the wine tank."

Derek shook his head. "But if someone dragged him into the wine tank, they would have had to put on the necessary mask in order not to die themselves."

"Where do you keep the masks?"

"Small office inside the warehouse next to the tanks," Derek said.

"Who knows about them?"

"Pretty much anyone who has taken a tour of the Malveaux winery and estate. It's part of the tour when we explain safety measures and how the winery runs."

"Right, and you would say that's what? A hundred thousand people or so a year?" Jonah asked with a sarcastic chuckle.

"Basically. And your friends that are staying for the wedding, how about them?" he asked. "Did you guys go over that on your tour the other day?"

Derek glanced at Nikki. "Not when I was with you guys," Nikki said.

"You know, now that you mention it, I don't think I did go over that. I had a lot on my mind at that point. Nikki's aunt had just called and said that she couldn't make the wedding, and there were tensions in the group, so I did the short run through."

"Hmmm. Well then, I can only assume that whoever murdered Kenny either works here, has a working knowledge of wineries, or did some serious snooping around before taking him out. I'm game, gang. Any ideas?"

"Maybe," Nikki replied.

"Maybe?"

Then Nikki filled both men in on her thoughts, theories, and a possible plan on how they might catch a killer.

Twenty

IT wasn't as difficult as it might once have been to convince Jonah that Nikki and Derek could be useful in helping him with his investigation. Jonah knew Nikki could be an asset and had the mind of an investigator. She asked good questions and came up with decent theories. She'd helped Jonah with a couple of difficult cases already. In the past Jonah had given her stern warnings to stay out of any of his investigations and let the cops handle it. But Nikki wasn't great at heeding warnings, be they stern or otherwise. Then he'd actually come to her last year seeking her help with a murder case, really wanting her assistance, and that's when he'd started dating Nikki's friend Alyssa. He'd asked Nikki more than once to consider going into police work and becoming a detective. It had crossed her mind a few times that maybe following in the footsteps of her Aunt Cara would be a good way to go, but at this point in her life she was content and, more than anything, wanted to start a family. It might not be the right time to go directly into police work, but indirectly . . . sure.

Jonah thought her plan sounded feasible, and tomorrow it would go into effect. But a few things had to take place first, and now, they were going into town and getting the necessary ingredients to prepare Simon's gourmet meal for the evening.

They drove to McKinley Street with Ollie in the backseat of the Range Rover. It was nice to do something so ordinary, considering the circumstances. The farmers' market in Napa was more like a mini festival, with vendors selling everything from fresh flowers to baked goods to olive oils and chocolates. It was a foodie's heaven. Nikki needed to find everything they'd need for the poblano sauce. She picked up the veggies to make one of her summer specialties—a mushroom/squash soup that had enough heat to it to nicely complement the sauce for the ahi. For dessert, they decided on some truffles from the Napa Valley Chocolate Factory. Nikki looked forward to her favorite, which were the chipotle pepper truffles, and she knew that Derek would remain traditional, sticking to dark truffles. They'd have to pick up the fish at the Osprey Seafood Market.

Derek had Ollie on the leash. By the time they made it over to the truffle vendor, a tray of tasters was set out for customers. Derek held one out for Nikki and she took a bite. "Mhhm . . . interesting. Curry. I never would have thought, but then again I always get the spicy truffles."

"You do like things a little spicy, don't you, baby." Derek smacked her lightly on the butt, chewing on the other half of the truffle. Ollie whined. "What? You need to go to the bathroom?" Ollie wagged his long tail. "I'm going to take him over on the grass and let him do his thing. I'll be right back."

"Okay. I just have to get a bunch of cilantro, and then we should be ready. You got a poop bag?"

"Yeah."

Nikki watched Derek take Ollie across the way to find an acceptable place to do his thing while she paid for the truffles and headed over to where she knew she'd find some good cilantro. While holding a bundle close to her nose she breathed in the delicate herb. She felt a hand on her shoulder. "That was quick," she said turning around, and then caught herself. It was Andrés. "Oh. Hi."

"Hello. How are you?" he asked.

"Good. Fine. Considering. What are you doing?" She glanced around his shoulder in part to see if Derek was returning and also to see if anyone was with Andrés.

"Some shopping."

"Of course."

"Nikki, I have to tell you something."

Oh, no. "No, I don't think you do."

"It's very important. I actually have to show it to you. You need to come to my place so you can see it. It has to do with the wedding and Renee."

"What?"

"I . . ."

"Hey, Andrés." Derek slapped Andrés on the back a little harder than he might a pal. "How's it going? I heard you were back in town."

Andrés reached out his hand and shook Derek's. "Good. Thank you. Yes, I am back for a little time."

"Great." Derek smiled, and Nikki knew it was his

phony smile. He held out a bouquet of flowers. "I bought these for you." He handed them to Nikki.

"Thank you. That was sweet." She glanced at Andrés.

"We better get going," Derek said. "We're making dinner for my brother."

"Of course. My apologies for your tragedy. Give your brother my best, please. Take care."

Nikki and Derek walked away with Ollie and their groceries. They never mentioned seeing Andrés, but the tension that surrounded his presence hung between them on the quiet ride home. Nikki knew she'd be going to see Andrés. She also knew that she wouldn't be telling Derek of her impending visit.

Twenty-one

DEREK was out on the patio grilling the ahi and veggies. Nikki was chopping and mixing the poblano sauce in the Cuisinart and refilling the guys' wineglasses. Violet was trying to sit on Ollie, who was more than tolerant. The dog just lay there as the toddler pulled on the Ridgeback's ears and climbed all over him.

Nikki handed Simon a glass of Chardonnay. They were hanging out in the kitchen. "How's the shoulder?"

"It hurts, but I feel lucky to be alive. That maniac almost killed me. I've been wracking my brain and pretending to play sleuth like you to try to figure out who hates *moi* so much that they'd want me dead. I mean really who would want to kill me?"

"I hate to tell you, my friend, but it's not you that anyone hates so much."

Simon raised his eyebrows. "Um, darling girl, I was

almost killed during your wedding, I'm thinking someone is not my biggest fan."

"Jonah found a photograph of me that the shooter left behind. He or she had crossed me out in red ink."

"Oh, my." Marco brought a hand up to his mouth. "Nikki, this is terrible."

"Um, 'scuse me, but getting shot in the shoulder is terrible."

Marco gave Simon a dirty look. "That bullet was meant for our Nikki."

"There's more," Nikki said.

"More?" they both said in unison. Violet looked up from where she was now seated directly on top of the dog and repeated her parents' word. "Mo? Mo!"

"Yes, more," Nikki said.

"What more could there be?" Simon asked.

"Derek's college buddy Kenny, the party animal, was found dead in one of the wine tanks this morning. Derek found him."

"Lord have mercy," Simon said.

Nikki nodded. "And Jonah also found a photo of Kenny in the church, also with his face crossed out. And both Derek and I have received some strange notes, texts, that kind of thing." She went on to explain about the newspaper clippings. "All of these things are signed with Moros Apate Thanatos."

"The fates or Greek gods of doom, deceit, and death," Marco said.

"Oh," Nikki replied. "Wow, I didn't know that. I'd planned to look up the meanings when I got a chance. Derek and I talked about it."

"What do you think it all means, and, wait! What do you mean Kenny was found dead this morning? And you've been receiving strange texts and whatnot!" Simon said.

"Your brother found him in the tank, and Jonah came by a bit ago and let us know that it looked as if he'd had a head trauma and that he'd been dragged into the tank. And we're fine. I knew you'd get upset."

Simon looked at her with his wounded-puppy-dog look.

Marco again brought his hand up to his mouth. "What are you thinking? Why would someone want to shoot you, Nikki, and murder Kenny? What is the connection?"

"That is the million dollar question," Nikki said. "The only connection that Kenny and I would have is Derek."

Simon pointed at her. "And if I know you, you're already looking into things, and my brother is going to completely come unglued when he finds out."

She smiled smugly. "That's where you're wrong, my friend. Your brother has taken up the position that if you can't beat her, join her."

"No!" they yelled.

Violet was smacking Ollie on the head. "No, no, no."

Nikki walked over to her and lifted her up. "Sweetie, you can't hit the doggie."

"Doggie, doggie, doggie, no, no, no!" she sang.

"No, the doggie didn't do anything wrong. Why don't you come in the family room and play with Elmo?"

"Elmo, Elmo, no, no, no!" she yelled out with glee.

Ah, the simple pleasures of a two-year-old. Nikki set her down and took out a handful of toys from the box she kept at the house, and spread them around the floor, hoping to save Ollie from any more trauma. Apparently the dog didn't see it the way Nikki had, as he got up and came over to where Violet was playing and lay down next to her. She leaned back into him. "Doggie, doggie!"

"Your choice, bud. You're a good dog." Nikki patted him on the head and went back into the kitchen, where the guys were talking quietly amongst themselves. "What's up? Why the covert whispers?"

"Marco just shared some interesting information with me that could be something, or might not."

Nikki sat down, grabbed the wine bottle, and poured herself a glass. She took a peek outside and could see Derek scooping the veggies onto a platter. "Do tell."

"The night of the rehearsal dinner, after you two snuck away, I was in the kitchen cleaning up," Marco said. "I went to dump the trash, and I saw two of Derek's friends outside talking. They saw me and stopped. I said hello and went about my business. It seemed to be a, how do you say . . . upsetting discussion."

"Tense," Nikki suggested.

"Very."

"Who were they?"

"The man who was killed and the wife of the one guy."

"Which guy's wife?" Nikki asked.

"Not the prissy one. The nicer one."

"Lily?" Nikki asked.

"Yes. It was her," Marco replied.

"Huh."

Derek entered the house, looking up at everyone with hot platters in hand. "What's brewing? I can tell by looking at all of you that something is brewing."

Violet called out, repeating her uncle, "Booing. Sumtin booing."

Nikki nodded at Violet. "You got it, kid. Something is definitely brewing."

Grilled Ahi with Poblano Cream Sauce
and Bonterra Chardonnay

Yes something is brewing at the Malveaux Estate and it isn't nice and pretty. In fact it's deep, dark, and ugly. It's good that Nikki likes things a little spicy, and Simon is all about the drama. A dramatic and spicy dish that works well with brewing and stewing is this delicious grilled ahi with poblano cream sauce. If fish isn't your thing, this cream sauce also goes nicely with grilled chicken. The chardonnay is a great fit for either fish or chicken.

Bonterra's Chardonnay has firmly adopted a style some describe as international, with less oak aging and a deliberate attempt to emphasize the freshness and crispness of their stellar organic fruit from Mendocino County. Most of the grapes for Bonterra's Chardonnay are harvested along a 12-mile corridor near the banks of the Russian River, and year after year offer characteristic green apple, baked apple, pear, and citrus notes in the wine. There's a touch of vanilla from the dollop of new oak, but Bonterra ages in mostly neutral barrels to let the fruit shine through. An initial impression of rich, buttery cream quickly turns to aromas of honey and lightly toasted almonds, followed quickly by tropical aromas of pineapple, citrusy lemon, and crème brûlée. The wine is refreshing on the palate, with a minerality that is both bright and clean, seductively drawing you into a vibrant tartness and lemon zest that is absolutely, positively Bonterra Chardonnay, vintage after vintage.

> *2-3 fresh ahi steaks or 4 chicken breasts—grilled*
> *6 poblano chiles*
> *1 cup chicken broth*
> *¾ cup butter*
> *4 oz (½ package) cream cheese, softened*
> *½ cup (2 oz) shredded cheddar cheese*

Place chiles on an aluminum foil-lined baking sheet. Broil chiles 3 inches from heat 8 to 10 minutes on each side or until charred. Place chiles in a heavy-duty, zip-top plastic bag; seal and let stand 10 minutes to loosen skins. Peel and seed chiles, discarding skins.

Combine chiles and broth in a blender or food processor; process until smooth.

Melt butter in a large skillet over medium heat, and stir in chile mixture. Add cream cheese and cheddar cheese, stirring constantly. Cook 2 to 3 minutes, stirring constantly, until cheeses melt.

Twenty-two

NOT again. Nikki hauled herself out of bed before the crack of dawn, feeling like a total jerk and then some. She'd had another dream about Andrés, and this one had been about the two of them in a house on a hill surrounded by vines. But they weren't the only ones in the dream. There was a child—their child—and the toddler kept repeating everything that the two of them said to each other. They found it amusing and kept saying how lucky they'd been to finally find each other again and how much they loved one another.

"No. I love Derek," she whispered to herself, as she looked back at him still in bed sound asleep. Ollie lifted his head and put it back down. He was not necessarily an early riser. He definitely wasn't a before the sun riser.

She went into the kitchen and made a pot of coffee, trying hard to shake off the dream. She knew dreams could really mean something. Was her subconscious telling her something? She refused to believe that it was telling her that she was in love with Andrés or that he was the one she was meant to spend the rest of her life with. She was in love with Derek, and he was who she was meant to spend her life with and have children with. The dreams were only occurring because Andrés had shown back up abruptly and right before she was supposed to be married. Maybe it was her guilty conscious she struggled with. An interesting thought entered her mind, and she tossed it out almost as quickly as it had weaved its way into her brain—Andrés *had* shown up right before her wedding day. She *had* broken up with him and not in the most decent of ways. Could he be far angrier than he'd let on? Could he be angry enough to strike out? No. No way. This was Andrés. He'd loved her. Claimed that he *still* loved her. He would never hurt her, and he certainly had no ties to Kenny. Today after the sun came up, she would go and see him as he'd asked her to. She would find out what it was that he wanted to tell her about Renee, or rather show her. She couldn't help but be intrigued.

She also knew that when she went to see him she would need to have a long talk with him and straighten out all of this turmoil, or whatever it was. Andrés really needed to move on.

But for now she couldn't think about it. She took her coffee into their office and booted up the computer. She figured it was long overdo to read up on her Greek mythology.

By the time Derek got up two hours later, she'd boned up on Greek mythology and did not like what she'd learned. The killer's call tag, *Moros Apate Thanatos,* translated into doom, deceit, and death. Great. This killer was one weirdo.

First off, as Marco had said the night before, *Moros* directly translated into English as doom or fate. He was the god who personified the end of every being, mortal or otherwise—according to Wikipedia. He was known to drive every being to their death. Supposedly this god was omniscient and omnipotent and not even Zeus could do away with him.

Apate was one of the evil spirits released from Pandora's box. There was nothing good about Apate. She was the daughter of Nyx, who was the goddess of night, and Erebos, who was the god of darkness. One of her siblings happened to be Moros. Her other siblings were just as awful, especially her brother Keres who was the personification of violent death and carnage.

Then there was Thanatos. Now here was a god who would make the skin crawl. He just flat out represented death, and no surprise but his folks were also Nyx and Erebos. He had a twin brother named Hypnos, the god of sleep. Jeesh, those Greeks sure had lots of kids. Most of his siblings carried negative connotations, including suffering, retribution, and strife, as well as deceit and doom. However, Thanatos was a god who was exclusive to peaceful death, while his brother Keres was the bloodthirsty one. Yet Thanatos was said to be merciless and indiscriminate. Now that sounded violent as far as Nikki was concerned. He was hated by and hateful toward mortals and deathless gods.

As the culture grew and changed, Thanatos was depicted as a more peaceful god and oftentimes drawn as a winged boy akin to Cupid. However, in modern times, he is depicted much of the time as a visage of the grim reaper.

Nikki also learned that "Thanatron" was someone who performed assisted suicides. Someone who saw themselves as a kind and generous human being who helped those who wanted to die, die.

Oh boy, they were dealing with a nutcase.

Now that she had all of this information, what did it mean? She'd need a psychologist or psychiatrist to help figure someone like this out.

It was possible that Alyssa could help her with this. Her friend had been taking psychology courses in hopes of earning her degree and being able to hang her shingle eventually in Napa. No matter what, there was something here with all of this reference to doom, deceit, and death, and Nikki aimed to figure out how it all connected to her and Kenny.

Twenty-three

NIKKI lied. Sort of. Omission wasn't technically a lie, right? Right? She told Derek that she needed to take Ollie in to have his vaccines updated. True. And she *would* go to the vet's. But she also planned to stop by Andrés' place and see what it was he needed to show her. She justified her omission with the fact that it would tear Derek up to know she was going to see Andrés. She had to go though. He'd indicated that he had something important for her to see. Something she didn't know, but she did need to find out. She figured sparing Derek and herself that turmoil was probably the smartest (and easiest) thing she could do.

This time there was no convertible blue BMW parked in front of his place, which sat back behind the Spaniard Crest winery. Andrés lived in the refurbished farmhouse on the back forty of the vineyard where he maintained a position as their winemaker. His own plot of land back in Spain had been planted, and Nikki knew that in a few years it would be ready for the first harvest. She'd had the chance to become Andrés' wife and build his winery alongside of him in Spain, but she'd turned him down and followed her heart, which had led her straight to Derek. She'd done the right thing. She had.

Andrés agreed to come back to Napa while his vines grew and were tended to in Europe. He would go back to Spain a few times a year to make sure everything was going as planned.

He was standing out on his deck. Ollie jumped out of the car and ran up to him, tail wagging. It was then that Nikki spotted a young chocolate lab who was lying at Andrés' feet. The puppy stood, dancing a little jig at the sight of one of her own. "See you brought your sidekick with you," Andrés said.

"Don't leave home without him. Who's this?" She bent over and gave the pup a rub, causing her to wag her tail at breakneck speed.

"This is Camilla."

"She's beautiful. When did you get her? How old is she?"

"Oh, she's Isabel's. I think she's about six months. I'm babysitting today. Isabel had to go into the city, so I'm playing uncle to her, otherwise my sister says she's known to eat the furniture."

Nikki laughed, again missing her friend.

"I'm thinking about getting one myself, but with the back and forth travel I have to do between here and Spain, it's probably not a good idea until I completely settle down."

"How is your sister?"

"Good. You need to go see her. I know she misses you."

Nikki didn't know how to respond. Isabel had initially claimed that she was fine with Nikki's decision to break the relationship off with her brother, but in the long run they'd drifted apart, with Isabel growing cooler and busier over time, until there was finally no real connection any longer.

"I'm pleased you came. I didn't know if you would," Andrés said.

"You said it was important and that you had something to show me that concerned Renee."

"I do. Why don't you come on in? Have some coffee."

She glanced behind her and spotted Ollie and Camilla leaping through brush. "I need to get him to the vet, so I don't have much time."

"All right then. Come on in. Let them play. It's good for the pup. I think she likes him."

"Looks like it." Nikki followed him into his house, richly painted in terra-cotta and turquoise. Andrés' house was warm, colorful, and had always felt good to Nikki. It was small but that had never bothered Nikki. It actually felt good, more cozy than anything else.

He pointed to a desk that had been built into his kitchen. She walked through the arch that led from the family room into the kitchen. A computer sat on his desk. "It's on here," he said and sat down and logged into the computer. Nikki stood next to him. A piece of his longish hair waved in front of his eye. She wanted badly to move it out of his face. She'd done that before—many times. She moved a few inches away. "Look here."

Nikki looked down at the screen. "Oh, my . . . What?"

It was a photo of Nikki from the wedding. She was getting out of the car, carrying her wedding dress and a makeup bag. Simon was next to her, along with Alyssa and Violet.

"There's more." Andrés flashed through more than a dozen photos of Nikki going into the church, standing at the entry before walking down the aisle. How had anyone gotten these, and furthermore who?

"Wait a minute, you said this had to do with Renee? Why do you have these? I don't understand."

"The day you were supposed to get married, Renee claimed she had to go up to Healdsburg and talk to a winemaker from Hungary for the book. I didn't think anything of it. She came back that evening, we had dinner, watched a movie, went to bed."

"Right."

"I got up to get some water around three in the morning, and she was up on the computer. I asked what she was doing. She said that she couldn't sleep and was surfing the Net. I told her to get off the computer and come back to bed. The next day when you showed up and things got chaotic, she flew out of here. Remember?"

"Of course."

"Well, when I got on the computer this morning, I accidentally put something in my trash bin and then realized I still needed the document. When I opened the trash file, I found this file with the photos."

"Renee took these pictures?"

"I assume so."

"Oh." Nikki needed to sit down and absorb the fact

that someone she considered a nemesis had come to
her wedding without an invite—someone who'd subsequently written that awful article, and someone who
might revel in her spending her wedding day in a morgue
rather than in the arms of a man who Renee had once
laid claim to.

Twenty-four

"DO you mind if I take these photos with me?" Nikki asked.

"No, I thought that you might want them. If I know you, you're trying to figure this all out. Here I can put them on a flash drive for you." He opened his top desk drawer and took out the flash drive and imported the photos onto it.

She smiled at him. Unlike Derek, Andrés had never really had a problem with her curious nature and her desire to right the wrongs of the world, or at least the wrongs in her world. "I am. Definitely I am. You can only imagine the havoc this has created for me. For Derek and Simon, our family."

"Yes." He clasped his hands together. "I am certain this is difficult. What is happening?"

"With what exactly?"

"With everything, I guess. Have the police any clues as to who shot Simon?"

"There are a few clues but none that lead to anyone directly. And it doesn't look as if it's Simon the shooter was targeting." Nikki told him all about the newspaper clippings and the photos, as well as Kenny's murder.

He instinctively reached for her hand and squeezed as a friend would. "No. Nikki, this is terrible. This scares me."

She didn't let go of his hand immediately. "Me too, but I want my life back." She pulled her hand away. "I have to go on with my life, and I don't see how that can happen until this person is locked away."

"Yes. And your marriage to Derek, then?" He left the rest of the question hanging in the air.

She sucked in a deep breath of air. "Yes. We will get married, but I don't know when that will be, and I think that any wedding we do have will be far different than what we'd originally planned. Much smaller, more intimate. I'm even for eloping, or just gathering my closest family and friends and being low-key. It has to be about the love and not all of the hoopla."

"I agree. Intimate is always what I saw for my own wedding. Maybe in Spain. Someday." He smiled. "There are beautiful rolling hills, covered in vines overlooking the land. That would be nice."

"Sounds lovely." She fidgeted and started to stand.

"Nikki, about what I said to you the other day . . ."

"I don't want to talk about it." She had planned to talk about it and ask him to move on with his life, but now that she was here with him, she simply did not want to talk about it.

"I need to. And I think you owe me that. Please."

She looked down at her hands. "I do owe you that much."

"Thank you," he whispered. "When you made your decision last year, I thought I could move on. I thought that I had. I wanted to, but then everywhere I would go, I thought I saw you. In a store. At the park. At a museum one day. Everywhere. And I dreamt about you."

Nikki couldn't look at him.

"Maybe I need more time."

She nodded.

"Or maybe it isn't over between us. All of these things that have happened in only a couple of days, maybe it means something. Maybe God, or the universe, whatever"—he swirled his hands in the air—"is trying to tell you something."

Now she took his hands. They were warm, calloused, and familiar. "I don't know that I can believe that. I know you want me to, but, Andrés, I love Derek. I really do."

He nodded. "But can you look me in the eyes, here and now, not like leaving me sitting on an airplane waiting for you, this is us together here . . . Can you look at me right now and tell me that you feel nothing for me? Can you tell me that you don't still love me?"

She sat there for several seconds without saying anything. Her mind racing with the past, and thoughts of the future. All sorts of thoughts and images and she actually felt physically dizzy as her heart raced inside her chest. She dropped his hands and stood. "I have to go. Thank you for the pictures and letting me know."

"You can't say it. Can you? Nikki, if you can't be honest with me, at least be honest with yourself."

She walked out the door and yelled for Ollie, needing

to get away from Andrés as fast as she could. Needing to avoid his questions. She had to wipe him and his questions out of her mind and her system for her own good, for his own good. She'd made up her mind about who she was going to spend the rest of her life with. Or had she?

Twenty-five

"HOW was he at the vet's?" Derek asked when Nikki and Ollie came into the house.

"Oh, you know, it's not his favorite place in the world to go."

"Yeah. I know. It sure took a long time."

"Yeah." It was all she could say. Did he know she'd made a detour and stopped off to talk to Andrés? Was deceit written all over her face? She wanted to tell him about the photos that Renee had obviously taken and explore what they might mean, but she couldn't do that. Not yet anyway. She knew she'd have to make a trip into the city and confront Renee herself.

"So I did what we talked about with Jonah," Derek said.

Still sort of in a daze from the conversation she'd had with Andrés, Nikki just stared at him.

"Uh, the phone call. *The Plan.* Although I really don't

think any of these guys had anything to do with it. But you and Jonah seem to think otherwise. Now it's your turn to put your part of the plan into effect."

"Right."

He came toward her and pulled her into him. His embrace was like coming home. She closed her eyes and tried not to get emotional.

"You okay, babe?" he asked.

That was all it took for the waterworks to begin. "I'm sorry," she said in between sobs.

He stroked her hair. "You don't need to be sorry for anything. Why are you sorry?"

She shrugged. "For all that's happened."

"Stop. Please. You don't need to apologize. We're going to get through this. I know it's difficult, but you know what I believe? I know when we get through this, life is going to get a helluva lot easier. It has to. This is simply a test to see how much our love can endure, and I know that we can endure anything that comes our way."

Oh, God, did she feel like a royal heel.

"No more tears. It's not like you. I know it's stressful, but it will be okay. It will all work out. I promise you."

"Thank you." She lifted her face and kissed him. "Thank you for being so wonderful and sweet and so damn smart."

He pulled away from her and bowed. "I'll take that." He laughed. "Now let's get back into this game so we can get back to life." He clapped like a coach.

"I kind of like this new you, all into getting the bad guy."

"I have my motivations." He smiled. "The sooner we

put this behind us and get to the bottom of it, the sooner you can become my wife. So make your calls."

"You got it." Nikki picked up the kitchen phone and called over to the hotel. Marco answered and connected her to Lily and Jackson's room where she left the necessary message, and then to Savannah and Tristan's, where to her surprise Savannah answered. Nikki could hear the wariness in Savannah's voice at the invitation, but by the time Nikki hung up the phone, plans were made for Nikki to have dinner with Savannah and Lily. A real girls' night out. Oh boy.

Twenty-six

NIKKI started the evening by pouring glasses of Syrah and serving baked lemon and mushroom crostini. She'd intentionally invited Savannah to the house twenty minutes earlier than Lily, feeling if she was going to get anywhere that she needed to do some damage control. Derek had planned to meet the guys up at the wine bar by the pool. They were each on a fact-finding mission. She knew this wasn't going to be easy for Derek, considering that these were his friends. More than ever, she wished that Simon was healthy. He made the quintessential sidekick. Marco had also helped her out in the past. He was Johnny-on-the-spot—always there right when she needed him to be and on top of things, but this time it was up to Derek, and her fingers were crossed that something would come out of the evening that might lead them closer to finding a killer.

Ollie remained in the house with Nikki, helping her

feel secure. One thing she'd discovered over the past few years in wine country was that murderers weren't always men. Men and women both committed murders, and she'd been unfortunate enough to, at one time, be alone in a room with a murderess. It hadn't turned out so well for the killer, but Nikki didn't want to take that chance ever again. At this stage of the game there was no way she could say that Savannah or Lily couldn't have taken Kenny out. Now shooting at her from the rectory was a whole 'nother matter since they were with other halves in the church. Their husbands certainly would have noticed if their wives were brandishing a gun and sneaking off inside the church to take aim at the bride. Unless they were in cahoots—a kind of Bonnie and Clyde thing. Hmmm . . . That would be a theory she would have to run through in her brain, but at the moment she needed to take the appetizers out of the oven. Her first guest was rapping on the front door.

When she opened it, she almost didn't recognize Savannah, who wasn't dressed in tennis whites or pearls, but rather a pair of jeans and plain white T-shirt. Her light blue eyes were red and her face a little swollen as if she'd been crying for some time. Her hair was tied back in a ponytail. She smiled weakly at Nikki. "I figured this was casual."

"Of course. Like I said on the phone, it seems all of us will be spending a little time together until the police have a chance to talk to everyone who knew Kenny and who was here at the time of the wedding. I thought that maybe we could get to know each other better. And I feel bad that we didn't exactly start out so great. I'm sorry about that. I think I really had wedding jitters, you know, and my nerves got the best of me."

Savannah nodded. Ollie finally realized there was a newcomer in the house, but he was comfortably seated on the sofa and so just lifted his head, made a low growl, and decided that the company didn't appear threatening.

"I have wine or water, soda, iced tea?"

"Anything stronger?" Savannah asked.

"Um, sure. What do you like?"

"Tequila."

"Oh. Okay. I actually make a good margarita. Derek taught me. It's all in the fresh juice. You have to squeeze your own lime juice and a little orange juice. It's very good."

"No. I just want tequila."

"Uh, sure." Nikki walked over to an antique liquor cabinet in the dining room. She took out a bottle of tequila and went into the kitchen where Savannah had taken a seat at the table. "Do you want it mixed with anything? Ice at least?"

"No. A shot glass will do."

"Are you sure?"

"Yes."

Nikki took out a shot glass from the cupboard and poured Savannah a shot. She set it down in front of her and before she could ask her if she wanted a lime wedge and some salt, the woman shot it back.

"Can I have another?" Savannah asked.

Nikki reached across the table and touched her hand. Yeah, sure, when Savannah walked in, Nikki's act at being nice was in order to gain information at some point in the evening—any kind of info that might help them out—but it was obvious the woman was hurting and regardless of how callously she'd treated Nikki, she knew it wouldn't be right to not show her some kindness. "I'm not sure what you're going through. It's obvious that you cared a great deal for Kenny, and this has really upset you." Savannah nodded. "But I think I speak from experience when I say that downing Patrón won't help for long. Maybe talking about it would be better. Like I said, I'm sorry we didn't get off on the right foot, but you and Tristan are Derek's friends and I think maybe we should try to make amends. I'm a decent shoulder to cry on."

Savannah sighed. "I suppose I was pretty much a bitch to you." She smiled through her tears. "It's just that . . ."

"Hello? Nikki?" Lily walked in the front door and Nikki stood to go and greet her. "The front door was cracked open."

"Oh." Nikki frowned. "I must not have gotten it closed all the way. Savannah is in the kitchen. Come on in and have a glass of wine or, uh, tequila."

Lily looked at her oddly, and then mouthed. "Oh." She pointed toward the kitchen. "Savannah?" she whispered.

Nikki nodded.

"Ah. No, I think I'm good with a glass of vino."

"Great. I also fixed up some appetizers."

"Sounds good. So what prompted all of this?" she asked as they entered the kitchen in time to spot Savannah setting her shot glass down. Nikki glanced at the bottle of alcohol and from the looks of it, Savannah had taken her one minute window of opportunity to down a couple of more shots. Taking Nikki's advice was something the woman apparently had no intention on doing. What Nikki didn't want was for Savannah to get so hammered that she wouldn't be able to answer any of her questions. A little alcohol was good for getting people to flap the lips. Too much usually meant they were under the table and would put an end to any sleuthing.

"Hey, Lil. Have some tequila with me, let's talk about old times. Nikki, why don't you bring over that photo album from the other day? And that annual. Look at us in our youth. Have I got some stories for you."

"Sure. Sounds good." Maybe Savannah was one of those people who became more alive when she drank. Starting with the past and with the photos did seem apropos to Nikki. Never knew what history might reveal about the future, and tonight Nikki had the feeling Derek's college days might give her some answers to what was happening in the present with a killer on the loose in Napa Valley.

Baked Lemon with Mozzarella and Mushroom Crostini

with *Bonterra Syrah*

It's a strange gathering happening at Nikki's place—what's with Savannah and the tequila? But something to make this get-together work to Nikki's benefit is an appetizer that is as interesting as it sounds—and delicious. Open a bottle of Bonterra's Syrah and enjoy!

Mendocino's Mediterranean climate has proven ideal for growing memorable Syrah. Warm summer days and cool, foggy nights (with temperature swings midsummer that can nudge 50 degrees) nurture the grapes until berries begin to senesce ever so slightly. In the Rhone Valley, tradition calls for blending with varietals such as Grenache. A variety of rootstocks and Syrah clones such as the Duriff and Estrella River are planted in soils that include Feliz Loam, Red Vine Sandy Loam and Yoykayo Sandy Loam. Bonterra's pick in small bins and ferment in small open-top fermenters. After completing malolactic fermentation, this vintage was aged for eighteen months in French Oak from a variety of coopers to assure a layering of flavors. They bottle and allow the wine to rest and gain complexity for several months prior to release.

Bonterra's Syrah vineyards, including the newer Biodynamically farmed Butler Ranch, which ranges upwards to 1600 feet above sea level and represents two-thirds of this vintage blend, are quite young, just teasing their prime growing years. You can see youth well served in the wine's brilliant crimson color and intense, heady aromas of black cherry and wild mountain blackberries before giving way to bitter-sweet, vanilla chocolate. The tannins are velvety smooth and supple. The oak is wonderfully integrated, with complementary flavors of cedar oak spice. This is a distinctive Bonterra Syrah, more fruit-forward than previous vintages, more distinctive and unique.

6 lemons, halved with flesh removed
1 lb fresh mozzarella, cut into small cubes
6 cremini mushrooms, finely chopped
3 tbsp fresh parsley, finely chopped
1 small shallot, finely chopped
1 tbsp olive oil
12 slices good rustic bread, toasted
Salt and pepper, to taste

Preheat oven to 300 degrees. Heat oil in a saute pan over medium low heat and cook shallots until just translucent. Add mushrooms and cook for five minutes. Remove from heat and mix with parsley and mozzarella. Season to taste and spoon into lemon shells. Place on a baking sheet and bake until mozzarella has thoroughly melted.

Remove from oven and serve with toasted bread, spreading cheese over the bread.

Twenty-seven

SAVANNAH told story after story about party after party and filled Nikki in on how they'd all met. Lily eyed Nikki a few times when talk turned to Derek and what a flirt he was.

"All the girls adored Derek. What isn't there to adore?" Savannah asked, slurring slightly. The petite woman could hold her liquor, and she'd lost some of her sad demeanor as she recounted the past. "Look at this picture here."

It was one that Nikki had already seen from a frat party where Derek was living it up with a pretty brunette. "Even Nancy was into him, but she'd never admit that because she was engaged to Zach already."

"I don't know that Nancy was ever into Derek," Lily said. "From everything I ever saw and knew about her, she was totally into Zach."

"Nancy? Zach's wife?" Nikki said.

Savannah nodded. "Soon to be ex-wife."

"What happened, do you know?" Nikki asked. "I mean with the marriage."

Savannah shrugged. "Same old same. You know, Zach was absorbed in his work and not emotionally available for Nancy. She had a couple of miscarriages and wanted to adopt, but Zach insisted they keep trying to have a biological baby. Then he lost his job as a pretty big exec at the ad agency he worked for. Nancy said he was kind of a sacrificial lamb for them because they were looking for a fall guy. Apparently it had to do with over-billing clients. I don't know. Then he poured their savings into starting his own company, and he's struggling to make it work, and she's just tired of it all. Probably why she went down to Puerto Vallarta. She loves it, and I know they have a vacation home there where she wouldn't mind living. She's an artist and into the Latin culture. Probably a good move on her part."

"Probably," Nikki agreed.

"I don't know. Mexico is still a third world country," Lily remarked.

"Have you ever been to Puerto Vallarta?" Savannah asked. "It's beautiful and there are a lot of ex-patriots down there. I think she'll do fine."

Nikki finished her wine and stood. "I need to get the chicken out." She'd made a Greek chicken—stuffed chicken breasts with olives, feta, red peppers, and pancetta. "I'll be right back."

"How did you wind up with Jackson?" Savannah was asking Lily as Nikki set down their plates.

"What kind of question is that? I love Jackson. He's a great guy. He's a great husband and a fantastic father."

"Yes, that's right. You were knocked up when you got married your senior year."

Lily frowned. "It happens, but that isn't why we got married."

"Uh-huh." Savannah laughed.

Her initial buzz seemed to be turning into drunk ass, with an emphasis on *ass*.

"What are you saying, Savannah?" Lily asked.

"I know," she leaned in over the table and whispered loudly.

"I don't know what you're talking about," Lily replied.

"I know that Kenny is the father of your oldest kid."

"What?" Nikki said.

Lily stared at Savannah.

"And I know that you refused for years to allow him to take a DNA test to prove he's the kid's father. You're something else. Here all Kenny wanted was to know his son and you made sure that wouldn't happen."

"I don't know what you're talking about, Savannah. I think you have me confused with yourself, because everyone, including your husband, knows that you've been screwing Kenny for years."

Twenty-eight

"WHAT? I didn't know that," Derek said, lying in bed next to Nikki later on that evening.

"Oh, yeah, it's juicy. And after Savannah made the comment about Kenny being Lily's son's dad, and then Lily shot back with everyone knows Savannah's been sleeping with Kenny on the side for years. Let's just say it got ugly. The claws came out."

Derek shook his head. "This is horrible."

"Savannah tried to smack Lily, but Lily is one strong woman. She had Savannah in a choke hold so fast I practically dropped the dinner plates. Then I tried to pry them apart, and it wasn't until I yelled at Lily to get a grip that she let go."

"Then what happened?" Derek asked.

"Savannah stormed out, and Lily sat down at the table and just sat there for a few minutes in silence. I didn't know what to do. Then she drank the rest of her wine. I offered her dinner and she ate a little bit. But get this, over dinner she did tell me that it was true."

"What! What was true? Wait, I think I already know. I can't believe this. She told you that Kenny could have been the father of her oldest son?"

"Pretty much. In fact, she and Kenny were arguing about it the other night. Marco saw them and he said they looked to be having an upsetting conversation. His words. Lily claims that Jackson has no idea about Kenny. But what if he does? What if he murdered Kenny in order to save his relationship with his son and his wife? Remember when we had dinner with them that first night? Well she went on about how proud they were of Jonathon, and especially Jackson."

Derek didn't reply.

"Honey?"

"I'm thinking," Derek said. "Over dinner with the guys he really didn't have anything nice to say about Kenny. Actually he called him an ass and then took it back when he realized we were all looking at him. Then he retracted and said that even though Kenny could act like an ass, that was what made him who he was. He was the life of the party. Those were Jackson's words."

Nikki pointed at him. "See, you're getting the hang of this." She got up and took a notebook off the dresser. "Start taking notes. Think about this. Jackson's comments are a little change from the other night when he was all about having a beer and hanging out in the pool with Kenny until Lily put her foot down. He seemed to enjoy the guy's company. Grab that notebook."

"Why me?" he asked.

"Because you have neater handwriting than I do," she replied.

"True. Okay. But for the record, I don't like this. These people are my friends."

"Yeah, well, one of your friends might be a killer."

He frowned.

"I'm sorry to be so blunt, honey, but it's true, and we have to figure out if one of them is. So start writing."

"Fine." He took a pen from his nightstand and opened the notebook.

"Okay, so we now know that Kenny was aware he could be the dad of Lily's son. Jackson might be aware of this. Lily certainly didn't like Kenny, and Marco told me last night over dinner he saw Lily and Kenny having a heated discussion out back the night of our rehearsal dinner," Nikki said.

"You didn't tell me that."

"I was fact finding, and I'm telling you now. My brain had to process the information and now it's all kind of making sense."

"Hmmm."

"Right. Those two have a motive to want Kenny dead. Each one could have killed him. Lily is one strong lady, physically. I think she could be stronger than Jackson. There is the possibility that they could have been involved in this together."

"What?" Derek said.

"Think about it. Let's play this out. Let's say that Kenny told Jackson that he'd slept with Lily back in the day, right? Jackson is mortified and goes to his wife who he obviously loves. She confesses and reveals that it's possible Kenny is their kid's dad. Jackson's entire life, his family, is threatened at this point. Whether or not Kenny was the kid's father, Jackson is the kid's dad."

"It does present a good motive, but let me ask you then why would either one want to take a shot at you? Why all the notes and weirdness?" Derek asked. "That doesn't make sense."

Nikki nodded. "No it doesn't." She sighed, and looked up at the ceiling. "Wait a minute though. Jackson and Lily don't strike me as stupid. Jackson rode over in the limo with you, right?"

"Yes. With me and Marco. Kenny was supposed to be with us. Tristan, Savannah, and Zach rode over together."

"Right. So did Lily drive over by herself?"

"I'm not sure, but I assume so."

"Maybe we should find out," Nikki said.

"What are you thinking?" he asked.

"That this could have been a well planned out plot. Start by sending us letters that sound like they come from a crazy person. Then one of them shoots at me— maybe Lily since she came alone, and maybe it wasn't intended to kill me. Maybe it was set up so that the cops would find the photos, which it obviously was. Kenny doesn't get found for a day afterward. There was a ton of chaos, so what I'm getting at is what better way to get away with murder than to create something so out of the ordinary, so insane, that there is no way it could look like the nice couple from upstate New York did it. If you were an outsider looking in, all of this stuff that has led to this moment would look like some serial killer was on the loose. It's certainly a decent decoy."

"Could be," Derek mused. "It could be."

"I know." She smiled at him. "And then there's your pal Tristan and his lovely wife. If it's true that Savannah was sleeping with Kenny over the years . . ."

"Wait a minute, though, that can't be," Derek interrupted.

"Why not?"

"They live on opposite ends of the coast."

"So. There are airplanes and alibis and all sorts of ways to get around that."

"I don't like that you sound like an expert in unfaithfulness."

"Shut up. You know that isn't true." An image of Andrés' face flashed through her mind. "I just know how people work. It could have been a once in a while thing. But if Tristan knows, as Lily insisted he does, then you have another motive."

"But, then, is the motive for taking a shot at you the same as with Lily and Jackson?"

"Maybe. But I can't discount Savannah. It's not like we hit it off, you know, and maybe she needed to end things with Kenny and maybe she decided before ever meeting me that she didn't like me. She was obviously tight with your first wife as well as Patrice. Then again, maybe all of this is way off base. Maybe it has something to do with Patrice and Adonis."

Derek brought a hand to his forehead. "My mind is spinning, Nik. This is crazy-making business."

"I know."

"I have a better idea."

"You usually do," she replied.

"Can we put away the crazy-making business and get down to some baby-making business?"

She grabbed the notebook from his hands and tossed it onto the ground. "I suppose that's an offer I can't refuse."

Twenty-nine

NIKKI woke the next morning to an empty bed except for a single pink rose and a note that read: *Had a thought and needed to check into it. Ollie is on porch keeping guard. See you in a while. Love you. D.*

What could that all mean? He had a thought about what? Interesting. Nikki noticed the notebook was gone. He must've thought he'd find something out and needed to take the notebook with him. Well, there was something Nikki needed to find out herself, and it was best that Derek wasn't at home to question where she was headed. She didn't know how long he'd be out, so she did her best to hurry and get ready. She also printed out the photos Renee had taken from the flash drive Andrés had given her. Photos in hand, she poured herself a cup of coffee and headed out the door. Opening it she took a step back when faced with Simon.

"Where you off to so early, Miss Bright and Sunshiny? I came for coffee."

"Oh, hon, I have to run an errand, but it's good to see you up and about. Where's Violet?"

"Marco was taking her to the pediatrician this morning for shots. I hate that trip. I don't like them poking on my little girl. Marco is the tough one. He can handle it."

"I understand. Well there's coffee in the kitchen and I'll be back later, so come visit."

"Uh-uh. Not so fast. Where are you going and what are these?" With his good arm, he shot out and grabbed the photos from Nikki's hand.

"Give those back."

Simon flipped through them. He clucked his tongue. "What do we have here?"

"Some photos from the wedding that didn't take place." Nikki smirked.

He took a step back and eyed her, eyebrows raised. "You are on a mission, aren't you?"

She sighed. "Yes."

"I wanna go."

"You don't even know where I'm going."

"So. I'm bored. I'm tired of daytime TV. I need some fun. Please let me go."

"It'll be awhile. I have to go into San Fran."

He smiled widely. "Yipee. Wish I could clap, but with my arm in this sling . . . Please take me."

"What about your arm? What about Marco and Violet?"

"My arm hurts." He pouted. "But some good food in

the city and maybe a little stop off at Saks will make me feel better."

"I'm not going shopping."

"You say that now," Simon replied.

"No. I'll tell you again—we're not shopping."

"Please, please, please. My arm . . ."

"You're terrible."

"I know. I'll call Marco from the car and tell him that you're taking me on a cheer-up drive into the city. He'll totally understand. But what are we really doing?"

"We're going to visit Renee Rothschild."

"No!"

"Yes."

"You mean that sleazy little snake who tried so desperately to slither into my dear old brother's life and take him away from you forever and ever?"

"That would be the one."

"Ooh, this sounds delicious. Let's go."

"After you." Nikki let Ollie into the house and, before long, she was on the road listening to Simon carry on.

As Nikki filled Simon in on what she knew, he shook his head like a Tasmanian devil on speed. "Whoa there, Nelly. You mean to tell me that Renee the snake was at the wedding and snapping photos of *you*?"

"Yup."

He closed his eyes and breathed deeply for a few seconds.

"What are you doing?" Nikki asked.

"I'm absorbing this information and tuning into my higher self. Intuition can lead us to the answers we seek."

"Of course," Nikki said. "And what does your sixth sense scream?"

"Shhh. I'm trying to connect with my spirit guide."

"Can I ask, who is your spirit guide?"

"It depends. I have a few. Now be quiet."

Nikki kept her eyes on the road. "Maybe I should get a spirit guide."

"Would you shut up?"

"That doesn't seem very spiritual—telling your friend to shut up."

Simon opened one eye. "Do you want the help of Tsu Lao Lizu, or not?"

"Sure. Whoever that may be."

"Tsu Lao is an ancestor of our little Violet. He was a healer in the twelfth century, and he has been one of my spirit guides for some time now. He led me to Violet."

"How come I'm just now hearing about this?"

"A relationship with one's guides is very, very personal, sweetie. I don't jabber on about them."

"Huh. Okay so what's old Tsu telling you?"

"Give me a minute, and this time I *mean* be quiet."

"Fine." Nikki tightened her grip on the steering wheel.

A few minutes later, with one long sigh, Simon said, "Tsu says that you must look at the obvious. What appears clear to you is not and what isn't, is."

"Ooh. That's helpful. So insightful. I can see how this spirit guide thing really works."

"Am I sensing sarcasm?"

"Uh, hmmm, okay, yes. Come on, what the hell does that mean? Look at the obvious? No shit. And then what looks to be clear to me isn't, and what isn't clear is? Simon, as much as I adore you, where do you come up with this crap?"

"You know I didn't have to come with you today. I don't need this abuse."

"You begged me to come!"

"Fine. Maybe I did. But you owed me. I was shot at your wedding. So let's talk about what Tsu says. These photos of you in all your splendor, well they are obvious, clear. Now, there are no photos of you after the chaos. Are you sure that Renee took the photos? Where did you get them? Who gave them to you? I doubt Renee did, or else we wouldn't be going to see her."

Nikki swallowed hard. "A friend gave them to me."

"What friend?"

She sighed. "Andrés."

"Andrés? Smoking hot Spaniard Andrés? Salsa-hot-on-you Andrés? Old flame, luvva, Andrés?"

Nikki shot him an "I'm gonna kill you" look. "First off, we never became lovers. And, yes, that Andrés."

"Oh, girl."

"Don't 'oh, girl' me."

"I only have one question, and one statement."

"No."

"Yes, I do. And you are going to answer me. How is it that you are in touch with your former luvva? And don't you know it is bad business to be talking to the former luvva while you are getting married to my brother?"

"Simon, do you enjoy getting on every one of my nerves?" She went on to explain how she'd come to be back in touch with Andrés. She didn't add that Andrés had mentioned he still loved her and that she'd been having dreams about him.

"I see."

"What does that mean?"

"What's clear here, or what may not be to you, is that . . . Well, let's start with what is clear. Andrés gave you the photos and *told* you that Renee took them. What may not be so clear but should be is that *maybe*, just *maybe*, it wasn't Renee taking those photos but Andrés! Have you ever thought about that? Maybe your former luvva is feeling jilted, and he decided to take a shot at you, literally."

Thirty

"YOU are ridiculous," Nikki said. "That's the stupidest thing you've ever come up with. Andrés doesn't want me dead. He loves me."

"What!"

Uh-oh. Cat outta the bag. She sighed. "He told me the other day that he still loves me."

Simon clucked his tongue. "Dear God, this is so, so, so seedy and *Gossip Girl.*"

"Right there, right on the last nerve," she warned. "It's not like that. I told him that I am in love with Derek and we are getting married. Besides, maybe Andrés did feel jilted, but why would he take out Kenny? And trust me, Andrés is no killer."

"No. He's a luvva." Simon fell into hysterics.

"Here's her office. No more jokes, no more Tsu Lao or whatever his name is, or any spirit guides for that matter.

This part of the discussion is over. Now do you want to help me or not?"

"I'll help you, but this conversation is far from over."

Nikki slammed the car door and walked toward the building of Rothschild Publishing. Being irritated didn't help one with the thinking process. How was she going to incorporate Simon into this little shenanigan? They stepped out of the elevator on the fifth floor. Nikki approached the receptionist's desk. "Hi. I'm here to see Renee Rothschild."

"Do you have an appointment?" An eclectic looking young woman with blue black hair asked.

"Yes." She lied. And gave the woman her name.

The woman scanned her appointment book. "I don't have you down."

"I know our appointment was today."

"Let me go and see Ms. Rothschild. I'll be right back."

"Tell her that it's very important."

The woman walked down the hall without looking back. Nikki hoped that Renee would see her. Knowing Renee, her curiosity as to why Nikki was there would get to her. She was right. A moment later, the receptionist came back and told her that Ms. Rothschild was in her office waiting to see her. She glanced at Simon. "Wait here."

His jaw dropped but he sat down on the sofa and picked up a magazine.

"This is a surprise," Renee said, standing up from behind her desk. As usual she was dressed to the nines, tall, tan, and beautiful. Perfection personified. "To what do I owe this visit?"

Nikki tossed the photos onto Renee's desk. "Can you explain these?"

She slowly picked them up and thumbed through them. "Looks like you on your wedding day."

"Right. The wedding that wasn't."

Renee smiled. "So sorry about all of that."

"Sure. Thanks. Why were you at the church that day and why were you taking pictures of me?"

"I don't know what you're talking about." Renee crossed her arms and sat back down in her chair.

"You're not going to sit there and tell me lies. This is serious, Renee. Simon was shot. He could have been killed. The police think that the bullet was meant for me. Now one of Derek's friends has been found dead at the winery, and I would think that the police might have some questions to ask you if they knew you were at the church snapping candid shots of me. Especially since it's a known fact that we're not exactly BFFs."

Renee's lower lip turned down and she placed her hands on her desk. "What friend?"

"What do you mean what friend?"

"What friend of Derek's was found dead?"

"No one you know. An old college buddy. I want some answers, Renee."

"Fine." She sighed. "I was not there. Okay. I wasn't. I sent a photographer in. One of those types that blends in no matter what. Hell, I figured you'd invited all of Napa and half of Sonoma."

"Why?"

"I wanted a story." She shrugged. "I had an idea."

"What do you mean you had an idea? What kind of idea?"

"I'm not permitted to discuss it," Renee replied.

"You're not permitted to talk about it? You send in someone to take photos of me that I'm not aware of, then chaos ensues, you write up your nasty gossipy piece, and now you tell me it has something to do with some idea you have and you can't tell me, but it involves me?"

"Bingo." Renee pointed at her and winked.

"I think you might want to rethink that, because if you don't start yapping, you can believe that when I leave here I will be going straight to the police, and I will tell them all about this."

Renee shrugged. "Go ahead. Threats make my day."

"You're a real piece of work," Nikki said.

"So I've been told. I'm busy. Here are your photos." Renee shoved them back across the desk toward Nikki. "See yourself out. Oh, and tell Derek *and* Andrés that I send my best."

Nikki stormed out of her office. Simon's eyes widened upon seeing her. "We're leaving."

He stood and followed her onto the elevator. "I take it that didn't go too well."

"I don't want to talk about it."

"You may want to take a look at this." He held up a newsletter.

"I don't want to read anything." They made it to the bottom floor and stepped out.

"You should read this," he said.

"Simon. No. I'm not in the mood."

"Just take a little look at the photo on this page." He turned over a page on the newsletter that read *Publisher's Insiders* at the top.

Nikki stared for a few seconds. "Oh my God."

"Told you."

She grabbed his hand and turned around, hitting the up button on the elevator.

Thirty-one

"WHERE did you find this?" Nikki asked, pushing the fifth floor button on the elevator.

"It was on the coffee table with all the reading material."

"This is huge!"

"Um, I sorta thought so, too," Simon replied.

The photo in the publishing industry newsletter was of Renee and a group of other industry players, many with drinks in hand. The caption beneath the photo read, "Island party in Coronado, CA during the *Publisher's Insiders* conference." It had everyone's name listed after that. Next to Renee in both the photo and written word was none other than Kenny Loughton. Kenny, Kenny. Derek's Kenny. And he was leaning his head on Renee's shoulder looking rather cozy.

"She knew Kenny, or at least this looks like it, and,

oh my God . . ." Nikki said stepping off the elevator and heading toward Renee's office.

The receptionist stood. "Excuse me. Yoo-hoo. No, no, no. Where are you going?" She trotted in behind Nikki and Simon.

"I left my purse in Ms. Rothschild's office."

"You have your purse. It's on your shoulder," the woman said.

"Oh, I-I . . ."

Simon stopped and held out his good arm. "Listen here, sister, Ms. Rothschild could very likely be involved in a crime. Or have been involved in one. See my shoulder here all bandaged up. Yeah." He nodded. "You see it. Well, little Ms. Rothsahootytooty just might be a wee bit responsible for it."

"I'm calling security," the woman said.

"Oh no, no. Call the cops for God's sakes," Simon said.

Nikki grabbed the good arm. "She's calling security on us, dumb ass. Now come on."

"Hey, there is no need for nasty words," Simon said.

Nikki opened Renee's office door. She wasn't there. She stormed back to the receptionist. "Where is she? Where did Renee go?"

The woman shrugged.

"After we leave here we will be in touch with Detective Jonah Robinson of The Sonoma County sherriff's department. And when my friend told you that Renee might have been involved in a crime, he wasn't joking. Now you can either tell me where she is, or mix yourself up in something you don't want to be mixed up in."

The woman sighed. "She's on her way to the airport."

"What?" Nikki shouted.

"Vacation."

"A vacation?" Nikki said.

"Yes."

"She didn't say anything about a vacation when I was in her office."

The woman shrugged. "All I know is she's been planning a vacation for a few weeks and that's where she's off to. A vacation."

"Where to? What airline?"

"Don't know."

"Liar."

"I don't know where she's going. She's private about that, and as far as an airline, she's probably flying in the company jet. That's all I know."

"Sure it is." Nikki stormed over to the elevator, dialed Jonah's cell number and got his voicemail. She left a message about what she'd learned about Renee and what had occurred. She tried to reach him at the office, to no avail, and she called Alyssa to see if she knew where he was, but she didn't answer the phone either. "Ugh." Nikki nearly threw the BlackBerry across the room.

Simon took her hand. "Chill, my sweet cherry pie. Anger is of no use."

"It feels like it could be of use right now."

"No. No. What you need is some retail therapy. Tsu Ling is telling me that is the truth."

Nikki growled at him.

"Very weird when you do that. I have asked you

already, no hissing. I'm going to include growling in that request. Now breathe. Good girl."

"You're so lucky I let you live."

"I know, darling. The feeling is mutual." He kissed her on the cheek as the elevator descended to the bottom floor.

Thirty-two

JONAH finally returned Nikki's call. She spoke at such a rapid clip that he had to ask her to slow down a few times.

"Relax, Nikki. I'll come by and get the photos from you and this newsletter. If there seems to be a connection, I can get a hold of the flight manifesto for Renee Rothschild and track her down. *If* I think she's somehow connected to Kenny's death and the shooting at the church."

"*If?*" Nikki shouted. "Come on, Jonah. First off, she has motive where I'm concerned. She sees me as a man stealer. When, in fact, Derek was always *my* man. On top of that, she was photographed with Kenny at a publisher's conference and they looked cozy."

"I understand all of that. But just because someone took a photo of them together and it looks like fun and games doesn't mean that Renee Rothschild had a motive to kill Kenny."

"But there's gotta be a reason. I'm sure of it. If you dig a little you'll find it."

"Maybe, and I will look into it. But right now, it doesn't warrant me bringing someone home from a vacation," Jonah said. "You have to understand that. I will look into all of this. Okay?"

"Fine." Nikki sighed. "When will you be by for the photos?"

"This afternoon."

"Good. I have some other information you might want to be aware of that I learned last night at my little soiree."

"If it's important, lay it on me now," he said.

Nikki told him all about the Lily/Jackson/Kenny scandal and the accusation that Savannah had been unfaithful with Kenny.

"Now that's all good. I will be prying into all of that, too. You can count on it. Good work. What about Derek? What did he find out, if anything, from his pals?"

"He didn't say much. I don't think he learned anything new. I also think that he doesn't want to believe it's possible one of his friends could be a killer."

"Right. Not many people want to believe such a thing."

Nikki told him that she'd see him later and hung up the phone. Simon was still with her. They were pulling into the winery drive. She'd convinced him that there was no time for retail therapy.

"Jonah on it?" Simon asked, still sulking at not getting to go to Saks.

"Says he is. I don't know. I'm sure he is."

Simon faced her. "I need you to do me a favor."

"What?"

"Drive up to the winery and help me get three cases of wine and then we have to take them to Max."

"Max?" Nikki asked.

"The hair designer."

"What! Uh-uh. No way. I told you we weren't giving him any wine. I paid him two hundred and fifty dollars already."

Simon pouted. "Nikki, I made a promise. Okay? The man did me a favor, and I know you don't like your hair, which I think is really totally adorable on you. You look like a little pixie. Like Tinker Bell. Oh my God! Oh my God! New nickname!" He clasped his hands together and looked heavenward. "That's it. That's it, Tink."

Nikki shook her head and pursed her lips together. There was no use fighting it. First it was Goldilocks, then Snow White, and now Tinker Bell. She took a deep breath in and let it out. "We're giving him the cheapest stuff we have."

"We don't do cheap, Tink," Simon said.

"Right. Come on. No, sit there." She parked the car around the side of the warehouse. "It's not like you can carry any cases anyway."

"That's not my fault you know. I didn't ask to go and get my arm practically shot off. But thank you. I need to call Marco and make some plans. We have a date night tonight. We were hoping you and Derek could watch Violet."

"Of course. But how about your mother and her brute of a husband? Isn't it hard to come home for any romance with those two lurking around?"

"Tell me about it. We're working on getting things straightened out. Hasn't Derek talked to you about it?"

"No. About what?"

"We're negotiating a settlement price with her to buy out the house and her share in the winery."

"Oh."

"Yeah, but there's a problem."

"What's the problem?" Nikki asked.

"You."

"Me? Why?"

"My mother will only agree to be bought out if Derek agrees to have you sign paperwork that gives you no rights to the winery, property, all of it, if there was a divorce or in case of Derek's death."

"What? She's crazy."

"She wants it all to go to Violet."

"I don't like the sound of any of this. Besides Derek will never agree to that. I'm going to be his wife."

"He told her that he would talk to you. She wants a prenuptial agreement signed."

"Oh, no. No. I'm sorry, but first off, where does your mother get off asking for that, and what is the big deal if she has no stake in any of this anyway once she's bought out? Does she hate me that much?"

Simon didn't reply.

"Stupid question. Of course she hates me that much. Huh. In fact, she might hate me so much that she could have wanted me dead."

"No, Nikki. I'll admit my mother is as cuckoo as 'one flew over the nest' cuckoo, but she's not a killer. I just can't believe that."

"Really? I can." She shut the car door and headed to

the back entrance of the winery, angry and frustrated. Why hadn't Derek discussed any of this with her? Was he seriously contemplating asking her to sign a prenup now? That just went against her grain, and not because she was afraid of divorce but because, to her, a prenup was a precursor that said that the possibility was there, and frankly, once married, she wouldn't even allow that possibility. Maybe she was old-fashioned. Maybe she was ridiculous, but those were her feelings and beliefs and she was sticking to them.

She located the cases of wine that Simon had promised Max and went into the office to sign them out in order to keep their inventory straight. Alyssa was busy inputting orders. "Hi," Nikki said.

"Hey. How are you?"

"I'm hanging in there. How about you? The other day wasn't easy on any of us."

"Good, but yeah it was really scary when Simon went down. It was surreal," Alyssa replied. "I was happy to see Jonah come home."

"I'm sure."

Nikki pulled up a chair. Simon could wait; he was in the air-conditioned car after all. "Maybe you can help me with something."

"I can try. What's up?"

"I thought that maybe you could help me compose a theory because of your psychology courses."

Alyssa crossed her arms and leaned forward in her chair. "I'm no psychologist yet, but like I said, I can try."

Nikki explained to her about the notes and how the killer had signed the notes.

Alyssa thought for a moment. "It's interesting. If I had to guess from what I know, I would say you're dealing with someone who possibly has an identity problem or has suffered a setback in regards to their identity. Maybe something happened that caused him or her to shake the perception of who they thought they were."

Nikki thought about what Simon had said about his spirit guide. As hokey as it was, Alyssa's points ran along the same lines as "what looks clear isn't always, and what is clear to the eye may not be as clear as it seems." A puzzle within itself.

"Taking it a little further though, gods and Greek mythology represent power. Right? It's possible that this person feels powerless and out of control by their shaken identity so they cling to the god persona to compensate for their perceived inadequacy. In this case, you're talking about two gods and a goddess, and each one of them is dark. It's not as if you're dealing with someone who calls himself Venus."

"Would you say then that he or she is now perceiving themselves as these three gods? That they have actually attached to the idea that they are doom, deceit, and death?"

"Exactly. You know how overly confident people, people with huge egos, go around talking about all that they do and accomplish, but on the inside they're very little? The substance isn't there at all. They tend to act authoritative and controlling when, in reality, it's a defense mechanism. It's a way to take on an identity as well as a certain set of skills. It gives this person a justification to kill."

"Yoo-hoo, Tink?"

"Simon," Nikki said, smiling at Alyssa. "I left him in the car. We're in here," she yelled out of the office.

"I don't have all day, Tink," he said peering into the office.

"Tink?" Alyssa asked, amused.

"Don't ask," Nikki replied.

"Can we get that vino and hop to?" he asked. He leaned over Alyssa and gave her a kiss on the cheek. "Hi, doll. You look smashing as always."

Alyssa rolled her eyes at him and looked at Nikki. "I know why you hang out with him. I look like hell—no makeup, T-shirt, and jeans—not exactly model material."

"You could wear a bag and look divine," Simon said. "Now Tink here . . ."

"Watch it. I might accidentally bump into that bad arm," Nikki said. "Come on, let's get the wine."

Alyssa helped Nikki carry the wine out, with Simon barking orders at the two of them on how to do it correctly. Of course they ignored him.

"Thanks for your input," Nikki told her. "I'm going to think about what you said and see if I can come up with anything."

"Anytime. I'm looking forward to seeing whoever did this in jail. Poor Kenny."

Nikki nodded and got into the car, pondering who might be just enough of a control freak or egomaniac to have pulled this off. She had some ideas.

Thirty-three

DRIVING out of the winery, Nikki spotted Zach and Tristan taking a walk. She stopped and rolled down the window. "Hi, guys. How are you?"

Tristan mustered a smile. "Taking a walk. It's beautiful out. My wife is sleeping in, and Zach was having lunch on the patio, so I asked him to join me."

Zach nodded. "How are you? Things okay? I know this has got to be really difficult on you."

"Things are okay. We'll get through this. We really appreciate you hanging around until Detective Robinson has a chance to clear everyone," Nikki said.

"Of course," Zach said. "Hey, Simon, how about you? How's the arm?"

"Hurts. But I'm alive. Thanks for asking," Simon replied.

"We have a delivery to make, so enjoy your walk. I think Derek is probably in the tasting room."

"We need to go see him then," Tristan said. "Take care."

Nikki pulled away. "It's after noon, and Savannah is still in bed? Not surprising after the way she tied one on last night at my place. She's an interesting one. You kind of knew these guys, at least through your brother, what do you know about Zach's wife?"

"Nancy?"

"Yes. I guess they're getting a divorce." Nikki turned the car back onto the highway.

Simon laughed.

"What's so funny?"

"It just doesn't surprise me at all."

"Really? Why?"

"Nancy was nice enough I guess, but just sort of crazy."

"Crazy how?"

"Oh, you know, Tink."

Nikki waved a finger at him. "No, I don't know."

"She was always an obsessive type, a little controlling. Artsy-fartsy chick, so the OCD crap really didn't make sense to me, but any time I was around those guys, she was a cling-on to Zach. He'd try to relax, hang out, but she wasn't having any of it. She was always around. Never gave the guy any space."

"Really? Savannah gave me a different picture. She made it sound like Nancy left Zach because he was a workaholic and didn't pay any attention to her."

"Maybe he didn't after being forced to for so many years. I'm just telling you what I remember of Nancy, and she was insanely jealous of Zach and his friends."

"What about Derek?" Nikki asked.

"What about him?"

"Savannah indicated that Nancy had a thing for Derek. That all of the women did back in college. However, Lily contradicted that statement," Nikki said.

"I would tend to listen to Lily. Now there's a gal with a head on her shoulders. I don't think Nancy had anything for my brother. I know Savannah did because we talked about that, and Savannah had a thing for anyone with a certain, uh, appendage, shall we say."

"Ooh."

"Yeah. Anyhoo, Lily, on the other hand, I always thought had a little crush on my big bro."

"No," Nikki said, glancing at Simon who arched his eyebrows. "Really?"

"I think so, but that is obviously so over. They have a slew of kids now and Jackson is a good guy."

Nikki parked in front of Maximilian's. "Here we are at the hair designer extraordinaire."

"Thank you, Tink." He leaned in and kissed her on the cheek.

"Sure, Peter Pan. At your service."

"Oh, I like that. I do. You are on to something there. I'll run on ahead and let him know we're here while you get out the wine."

"You do that." Nikki carried in each case one at a time. Twelve bottles of wine certainly wasn't a light load. When finished, she spotted Simon seated in Max's chair getting a haircut, bleaching his already white blond hair, *and* sipping champagne. "Simon," Nikki said walking over to him, "what's going on?"

"I see her intellect hasn't changed since our last encounter." Max tossed his hand around in the air, scissors waving. "But she is a divine looking creature. Really, darling, who does your hair?" He laughed.

"Funny." Nikki eyed Simon who smiled.

"Tea, coffee, champagne?" Max asked.

"No, thank you. Simon!"

"I needed a touch-up. The roots are growing back."

Nikki huffed, "Impossible. I'll go sit down and wait."

Stewing at Simon, Nikki took a seat at the front of the salon. She thumbed mindlessly through a couple of magazines. She picked up one titled *CA*. It was a new magazine all about the happenings and goings on in California with a focus on the glitz and glamorous.

While reading through it, she hit a section on socialites. Her stomach sank and her breath caught when she spotted a picture of Patrice and Adonis. The caption beneath it read, "Mother and son at opening for Hypnos Club in Hollywood? No! That's Patrice Malveaux of the Malveaux Wines Dynasty and her much younger new husband, Greek god Adonis Diodorus. Hmmm . . . wonder what he might be after?" Nikki couldn't help snickering. Wow. Whoever had written that caption hadn't been too kind to Patrice. Whatever. The woman deserved it, trying to call all the shots. Nikki flipped to the front of the magazine and about dropped it when she read who the editor as well as the publisher for it was. None other than Kenny.

Thirty-four

"SO Kenny knew Patrice and Adonis. Well, he didn't know them per se," Nikki said. She was seated across from Derek at the wine bar having a glass of Merlot and eating a beef tip salad. They were waiting for Simon and Marco to bring Violet by. They planned to take her for a walk and head down to the house. They had finally had a chance to meet up after the crazy day. "But he knew *of* them and look what he or his writer wrote. Did you know he published this magazine?" Nikki asked.

Derek set down his wine and took a look at the magazine. "I knew he was starting some new ventures. He did mention the *CA* magazine because he said that he wanted to talk to us about doing something with the Malveaux Winery and possibly the wedding in the 'Happenings' page."

"Well, he got Patrice and Adonis in the 'Happenings' page, and I can only imagine her reaction upon seeing it."

He shook his head. "Yeah. I'm sure she wasn't too thrilled with this, if she even saw it."

Nikki took a sip of her wine. "Of course she saw it. I'm sure she did. Do you know what this means? It means that Patrice, who we know has no love for me and wouldn't likely think twice if I was six feet under, could have a reason to want Kenny dead. It's why she came back here and brought her thug with her. What do we know about this guy? Look, it makes sense. He's Greek. They met at a Greek mythology class. He's strong enough to hit Kenny over the head and drag him into the tank. Plus, Patrice would have known to tell him to put on the mask before dragging Kenny in there. She had to have thrown a fit when she saw this." She pointed at the photo. "Plus the notes are all signed with the names of gods of fate. Weird. And I talked to Alyssa about that whole thing with the gods of fate. She says it's likely someone with some control and ego issues. That fits Patrice to a tee."

"You could have something, but I have a question."

"What?"

"Why would this Adonis be so forthright in telling you that he and Patrice had met at a Greek mythology course? Doesn't that seem strange? If they were the ones sending us those messages, that's a tip-off."

"Not all criminals are smart, honey. In fact, most aren't. Most screw up somewhere. I have a feeling that Adonis is simply a trophy for Patrice."

"You're right there, I'm sure. I don't know, though."

Nikki took a bite of her salad. "What about you? This

morning you left me that note about checking into a hunch. What was your hunch?"

"Oh, nothing. It didn't pan out anyway."

"Well what was it?"

"I was just trying to make some connection between you and Kenny. The only connection is me, so I was trying to figure out who might have some type of vendetta against me."

"Okay. And did you?"

"Not really."

"Must be nice not to have any enemies." Nikki laughed. "Lord knows I have plenty."

"I'm sure I have them. I do think your ideas about Patrice and Adonis are good. Did you tell Jonah about them yet?"

"No. He was supposed to stop by the house so we could talk, but I haven't seen him. I left him a message when I was stuck at that salon with Simon."

"He came by. I was there."

"Oh. Good."

"He said that he was going to get some photos that you said Renee Rothschild had taken from the wedding. I didn't know where they were, so I told him you'd be in touch. When did this all come about? How is it that Renee was taking pictures of you at our wedding?"

Nikki clucked her tongue, and gave him the need to know information that Renee had taken the photos and that Nikki had gone to see her that morning and now she'd flown the coop.

"Interesting. How long did you know about the pictures?"

"Oh, I had them for a day." She reached across the bar and poured herself another glass of wine and refilled his glass.

"We talked about all of this last night in bed. Why didn't you mention it to me?" he asked.

"I don't know." She shrugged. "Maybe because she was an ex-girlfriend."

"Nikki, we're questioning friends of mine that I've had since college. I think I could get over the fact that you might have some suspicions about Renee."

"Right." She smiled.

"What are you hiding from me?"

"Nothing. I'm not."

Simon and Marco walked up, saving the day for Nikki. "Hi, love bugs. Here's our doll baby."

"Thank you for taking care of her. We are going into town for some dinner, but we won't be late." Marco handed Violet over to Nikki and kissed both of her cheeks.

"Hair!" Violet shrieked and then laughed.

"Yes, baby, my hair is all gone," Nikki said.

"Did we interrupt something?" Simon asked eyeing Derek.

"No. Nikki was just telling me about the photos that Renee Rothschild had."

"Oh, yeah. Thank God Andrés gave them to Nikki, otherwise we'd never have known about that. Good thing the guy still has it bad for Tink. Those photos might lead us to the killer."

Nikki shot Simon a look that could kill. Simon frowned, realizing what he'd done.

Derek looked at Nikki. "Andrés?"
She closed her eyes. "Yes."

Asian Beef Tip Salad

with Bonterra Merlot

That Simon can't keep his mouth shut if his life depends
on it. Nikki's in a pickle now. Probably won't be able to
eat for a while with all of this upsetting and stressful turmoil. Good thing she'd shared that Asian beef tip salad with
Derek and had a glass of Merlot, before Simon opened up
the flood gates.

This recipe is tasty, easy and makes an excellent summer dinner meal. Pair it with Bonterra's Merlot and it's a
match made in heaven, or at least by the gods of fate—the
nice ones that is . . .

Biodynamic Merlot from Bonterra's estate McNab
Ranch comprises a little more than a third of this vintage
blend, with good representation from dependable Mendocino vineyards. McNab exists deep in a valley that's a bit
off the beaten path, and it was first certified for biodynamic
farming by the Demeter Association in 1996. The vines in
many blocks are relatively young, in loamy soils that are
well drained. Averaging 800 feet in elevation, most blocks
are high enough to experience the wonder of a Mendocino
day, where temperature swings can vary by 50 degrees.
Rootstocks vary by block, and Merlot clones 3 and 181
dominant, providing a real focus to the wine. Fruit from

this ranch makes it easy to defend the notion that organic farming makes for better tasting wines. Bonterra's blend for the vintage layers Merlot with Zinfandel and touches of Syrah and Petite bringing complexity and a slight smoked herb aroma to the wine. The heritage of Bordeaux is evident here. Aromas of black plums and dark cherries alongside cranberry, and cola spice adds to the somewhat old-world style. Medium full, even a bit creamy in the mouth, the evident ripeness of the fruit is somewhat restrained, leading to an unexpected elegant style.

1 head of red leaf lettuce
¼ red onion, thinly sliced
½ red pepper, thinly sliced
½ green pepper, thinly sliced
½ small container (or more) of grape tomatoes, cut in half
1 pickling cucumber, peel on, chopped
1 big handful fresh cilantro, roughly chopped
1 lb beef tenderloin tips

Season the beef tips generously with salt and pepper, and either grill or cook in a skillet over med-high heat until medium rare.

Mix vegetables together with the beef and then toss with dressing (recipe below.)

½ cup soy sauce
¼ cup rice wine vinegar
¼ cup vegetable oil
1 teaspoon sesame oil
1 tbsp chopped fresh ginger

2 cloves chopped garlic
1 tsp Thai chili sauce or other hot sauce
1 squeeze lime juice
1 tsp honey
Salt and pepper to taste

Whisk all ingredients together and store any extra in the refrigerator.

Thirty-five

"SINCE when do we keep secrets from one another?" Derek asked that night, lying in bed.

Nikki knew this moment had been coming all evening. They couldn't discuss the Andrés angle until after their babysitting duties were over. Simon had done a nice job trying to deflect the information he'd revealed by telling them all about Violet's favorite new thing to do, which was finger paint. He'd packed a set of finger paints and paper in her diaper bag, and all evening, Nikki and Derek had played the good aunt and uncle by doing artwork with Violet and trying to avoid the one topic they knew was coming between them. "Look, I knew this would be your reaction."

"And what reaction is that?"

"You're upset with me, and I don't really know why. You have no reason to be. Don't you trust me?"

"I have no reason to be upset with you? You go and

see an old boyfriend, not once but twice now without telling me, and you wonder why I'm upset. Of course I trust you, but when you keep things from me, I have to wonder if there is something I should be distrustful about."

"That's ridiculous." Ollie slinked out of the room sensing the tension.

"Is it?" Derek asked. "And what's this? That he's still in love with you?"

She shook her head. "Come on. That's Simon talking. You know how your brother is."

"I do. He can't keep his mouth shut, but he also isn't a liar."

"Maybe not a liar," Nikki said, "but he sure can exaggerate. And he didn't say love, he said he still had it bad for me."

"Same thing and you know it, and something tells me the guy is still in love with you and you know it. I don't think my brother is exaggerating about this though. I know how close you and my brother are, and that kind of information came from you. Did Andrés tell you that he still loved you?"

Nikki didn't answer.

"He did, didn't he? I'm gonna kill him. I'm going to kill him."

"Stop it!" Nikki yelled. "The green-eyed monster is ugly on you. It is! Now, I love you. I was marrying you. I chose you. I don't think you getting all stupid is a good answer. Andrés will move on, but you need to drop it, too. Enough. And you know what? Since you're all high and mighty about secrets, how about the fact that you haven't told me that Patrice wants me to sign a prenup?

That's the only way she'll sell her shares and leave this place. Yeah, Simon spilled those beans, too."

Derek stood up out of bed. "Of course I was going to tell you. I hadn't because we really haven't had time to talk much other than about the murder."

"Really? We share a bed. So what was your plan?"

He sighed. "I planned to talk with you, and I also planned to rip up the prenup as soon as Patrice was gone. You know I wouldn't hold you to something like that. I did plan to tell you, but did you plan to tell me about Andrés?"

"I didn't see the need to tell you about Andrés. The fact is that he provided me with information. I can't help his feelings toward me, but I did tell him my feelings for you."

"You should have told me," he said.

"Yes. I guess I should have, and I'm sorry."

Derek began pacing the floor.

"I said I'm sorry," she said again.

"I know, and I'm sorry, too. And you know what? This has made me realize that we can't have any secrets. None. We're supposed to be partners, and relationships are based on honesty. Good relationships anyway."

"We have a good relationship," she said.

He stopped and faced her. "I think we do, too, and that's why I have to tell you something. No more secrets." He sighed.

"What are you talking about?"

"I'm talking about eighteen years ago."

"Okay." She sat up.

"Me. Lily. I . . . one night, I . . ."

"Oh my God," Nikki said. "You slept with her."

"Yes," he whispered.

Thirty-six

DEREK'S revelation threw Nikki into a tailspin. Upset, confused, and considering what he'd told her to be more than just a simple secret he'd been keeping, she'd packed a bag and driven a half hour north to Calistoga where she checked into a room at the Calistoga Ranch. She needed to go somewhere where she could get away and think. Derek couldn't understand—or acted like he didn't understand—why this was such a big deal. He felt the past was the past and he'd left it there a long time ago. He'd begged her not to leave, tears in his eyes as she'd loaded up her car. She turned to him when he came running out after her.

"What does this mean?" he asked. "You can't go. You can't give up on us. That was the past, and I had to tell you because it could be why someone tried to kill you. You have to stay here with me, and we have to work through this together."

"I don't know what any of this means. All I know is that I have to go somewhere where I can think and be alone."

"Nikki, please."

"Please what? I have to think. I can't do that around you. I can't understand why if you did this with Lily in the past why you would even have this long-term friendship with Jackson. It's not right. All I know is if I slept with a friend's boyfriend, I could never show my face to that person again. And if I'm reading this correctly, you may actually be thinking that you're their oldest son's father."

"I don't know." He bowed his head. "Look, it was a big mistake. It was huge. It was college. We were partying. It was stupid. I hated myself for it, but Jackson has never known, and I love the guy."

"You didn't love him enough not to sleep with his wife."

"They weren't married."

"So that makes it okay?" Nikki asked.

"Of course not. I was an idiot. It was a mistake."

"Seems like you made quite a few mistakes in the past, Derek. What about Savannah? Oh, a little kiss was all. And now Lily. Did you make it a pastime to go around sleeping with your friends' girlfriends?"

"No! Of course not! Nikki, be reasonable. Let's talk about this."

"I told you that I can't. Not right now." She started the car and pulled away, tears blurring her vision. She angrily wiped them away.

Now, drinking a strong cup of coffee, she sat out on her hotel room balcony, which overlooked an olive tree orchard and a stream running through the valley. The sun was coming up and she welcomed it, not having slept all night.

Okay, so Derek claimed that sleeping with Lily was a mistake. Duh. How does one justify sleeping with a friend's girlfriend? And what about Savannah? Had they only kissed like Derek insisted? Could Nikki ever really trust this man? Sure people made mistakes, but his were huge and costly . . . And talk about keeping secrets! What was she supposed to do, and think? She loved this man. She really did. Only a few days earlier she had been supposed to marry him, and now she didn't know if she even knew him. Maybe he'd been one of those party guys, a frat guy who liked to score notches on his bedpost. But shouldn't friendship have meant more to him than it obviously had? Nikki had to know how that night had gone down eighteen years ago. It would be the only way for her to discover if she and Derek were meant to be. At that moment she couldn't think of a scenario that would even remotely make what had happened in the past okay. But she prayed for one.

There was only one person she could go to in order to get straight answers and that was Lily. The only thing about going to Lily with this information was that Nikki would be laying all her cards out on the table. What if Derek had been right the night before? That maybe Lily had wanted to get rid of Kenny thinking he was possibly the father of her son, and then harming Derek in some way. This begged the question, why would she not just go after Derek rather than Nikki, unless she was jealous of Nikki. People killed over jealousy. Sick but true. Or, maybe it was a way of getting even, or maybe it was

Jackson who'd targeted both Nikki and Kenny. Kenny didn't have a significant other, so he became the direct prey, and by killing Nikki, Jackson would have taken Nikki from Derek, in a different manner than the way Derek had taken Lily, but on some weird level it was conceivable that Jackson felt this was his right. All of it boggled her mind.

And the theory of broken identities and connecting to the three gods of fate? It was possible that Jackson had been powerfully affected by thinking for years that he was this kid's father. He identified himself as that and now he was feeling like he was losing control. Jackson didn't strike her as a killer, but maybe changing his identity when he did kill helped him to justify his actions. Lily could also fit into that category. If light was shed on lies she'd kept for years, it could also throw her into a tailspin, disconnecting her from that "perfect mother" moniker she seemed to identify herself with.

Nikki wasn't certain if any of these theories would pan out. What she did know was that her relationship was on the rocks and a killer was still out there. She also knew that Derek did love her and she did love him. But was love enough this time?

That wasn't a question she could answer, but there were answers for some of her questions. And even though she could be handing herself over to a murderer, she had to know the truth.

Thirty-seven

LILY met Nikki in the Calistoga Ranch restaurant for lunch. Derek had left several messages on her cell phone begging her to at least call him and let him know where she was. She'd finally texted him and told him she was fine and staying in Calistoga. She knew he'd be calling around looking for her. He texted her back asking her to come home, but she told him she wasn't quite ready and to please respect her time alone.

"You okay?" Lily asked. "You look a little tired. I was surprised that you called and asked me to meet you for lunch up here."

"I'm not going to waste time," Nikki said. "I am tired, and I need answers."

Lily looked at her oddly and replied, "Okay."

"I know about you and Derek. That you slept together in college."

"Oh."

"He told me," Nikki said.

Lily nodded.

"I also know that you were arguing with Kenny the other night."

"I already explained when I had dinner at your place what was going on with Kenny. I hope you won't tell anyone, because Jackson doesn't know, and I've thought about it and realize that it gives me a motive to have killed Kenny," Lily said.

"Yes, it does. And now with this revelation I've learned about you and Derek, I do believe it also in some roundabout way gives you a motive to try to take me out as well."

Lily took a sip of her water. "I didn't kill Kenny and didn't try to harm you. I swear. You have to believe me. And you can't tell anyone this, because I'm afraid it would devastate Jackson."

"Lies devastate people, Lily. I'm not going to tell your husband what you told me, but the police may find this out on their own. They have ways. I do need to know about that night with Derek, and I have to know if you think he could be your son's father, because he brought that up, too."

"Derek is not Jon's father. I know that." She sighed and covered her eyes momentarily with her hands. "That night . . . um, it was one of those things that happen. I, well, Jackson had left school that semester. Did Derek tell you that?"

"No."

"Jackson's ex-girlfriend, the one he'd had all through high school, tried to kill herself, and, uh, she tried to put that on Jackson. His grades plummeted and she kept calling and obsessing over him. He finally decided to go home for a bit and see if he couldn't straighten things out. You can imagine how I felt. Here this psycho girl was working my boyfriend, and he was falling right into her trap. And he fell further. He didn't stay in contact with any of us, and every time I would call, he'd be brief and I got fed up. One night I got drunk and wound up with Kenny. I actually wound up with him a lot. I fell for him, believe it or not, but he could never be serious with me, and he insisted no one could know about us. He had to keep up that reputation of his, you know, as the party animal." She smirked. "But recently he contacted me. He'd met someone, and they were living together. I guess they wanted a baby, and she couldn't get pregnant. Things went downhill, and she moved out of Kenny's place. Then he saw the announcement about Jon's graduation, and he started thinking that maybe Jon could be his son. He got weird about it. He insisted I have a DNA test. But come on, how unfair is that? I told him no way and that he wasn't Jon's father and he had no rights to him. He thought he needed to have a son, someone who looked like him, someone to carry on his name. He's our son. He wasn't Kenny's and he never would be, not in the way that Jackson is a dad to Jon, no matter what. I begged him to leave us alone. I was really upset to see him here."

"I'm sure you were, but what happened with Derek back in school?"

"I got mad at Kenny when he treated me like a second-class citizen. I was good for a late night call but nothing else. And you could say that Derek was always the guy to go to when in need of solace, but I went to him with a plan. I planned to seduce him."

Nikki found herself making fists.

"I was hurt and angry at both Jackson and then Kenny, and let's face it, everyone knew Derek was a nice guy. He was the real catch of the bunch. I told him my problems with Jackson, and he said he hadn't heard from him in weeks. I tried to get him to drink with me, but he only had a few beers. This will sound crazy and it probably was, is . . . but I had a friend who'd given me something to relax me. I don't even know what it was, but I slipped it in his beer and he started to relax a little. I tried to go in for the kill so to speak, but he just kind of laughed me off and told me that I was being silly, that we were friends. I decided to fast-forward my plan and went into his bedroom and changed into something slinky. I came out, and he was passed out on the couch. So I undressed him, which wasn't easy, wrapped myself around him and in the morning convinced him that we'd been together."

"Why?"

She shrugged. "I don't know. Maybe I thought if it got out then Jackson would be jealous. I was trying to get even with him for leaving me in the lurch, but then Jackson came back and we worked out our stuff, and well . . . I was already pregnant when he came back to school. I couldn't tell Derek what I'd done. I felt it was best to leave everything alone."

Nikki slammed her hands down on the table and felt the heat rush to her face. A group of women lunching at a separate table all turned and looked. "You have to tell him the truth. For all these years Derek has believed that the two of you slept together. And now it's come between us."

"Oh no! You can't let this come between you. Derek loves you. He adores you. I've never seen him this happy. It was me. It was all my mistake and my stuff. I'm sorry. You have to go and work this out with him."

"You have to go and tell him the truth. You owe him that. You owe me that."

Lily nodded. "I guess I do."

"And you're sure that Jackson doesn't have any idea that any of this could have gone on? Is there any way that he might think that you and Derek slept together?"

"No. I-I, well, maybe. But I really don't think so."

"Maybe, though? Maybe what? How?"

"Savannah."

"She thinks this happened between you and Derek?"

Lily nodded. "Well, I didn't tell her directly, but I did tell Nancy, Zach's wife or ex-wife, whatever. We were friends and roommates and she knew my plan, and I told her it happened."

Nikki was speechless, which didn't happen often. "I feel like I'm in the middle of a soap opera on speed. You need to straighten this all out."

"I'll do what I can."

After Lily left, Nikki ordered herself a glass of Zinfandel and dialed Jonah's number. This time he picked up on the first ring. "Have I got a story for you," she said.

"That makes two of us," he replied.

Thirty-eight

"AN unauthorized biography?" Nikki about yelled the words. "She can't do that!"

Jonah was sitting across from her sipping iced tea and nodding his head. "Sure she can."

Nikki was on her third glass of wine on an empty stomach. "That Renee! She's, she's, she's a bitch!"

"Slow down there, missy. I think you should eat something."

Nikki waved a hand in the air. "You know what, eating is overrated, and after what I've been through this week, I think getting a little buzzed, no, shit-faced, is in order. Yup. Totally shit-faced."

Jonah shook his head. "You're on your way there."

"Good. But listen, I'm gonna sue that Renee Roth-schild. Now how did you get this little bit of information?"

"Her plane landed on the big island of Hawaii

yesterday, and I called her up and questioned her. She wasn't too pleased, but I asked her about you and the photos and the wedding and her snide remarks to you."

"Oh, yeah, I bet she was so forthright."

"Actually she was. Then I asked her about her relationship with Kenny, and she claimed that she didn't even know the guy and she didn't even know he was dead. I faxed over the picture to her from that newsletter. She says that he was just some guy that she met at the conference who was hanging out with a group of them."

"Convenient. Isn't that just so convenient?"

Jonah set his tea down. "I didn't get the feeling she was lying to me."

"She's a sly one. Let me tell you. Real sneaky, snaky, snarky sly. That's her." She pointed at him.

"I don't think she's the one we're looking for, but I do find what you've told me about this Jackson, Kenny, Lily, and now Derek, angle interesting."

"Don't go telling anyone." Nikki felt those annoying tears again.

"I'm a detective, but more than that, I am your friend. I'm not going to air dirty laundry. I do think you need to sleep off your wine and go home and talk to Derek though. The man loves you. And you love him."

"Yeah."

"Don't 'yeah' me. Listen to me for once. Do that. I'm going to go and talk to Derek's friends again. I'd also like to have some more words with Patrice and Adonis."

"Definitely. Those two are bad news. Scary bad news." She nodded. "That Greek guy is all muscle. Now Patrice could have done this, but only with Bruto's help. Think about that one. She gets trash-talked in Kenny's magazine. And she *hates* my guts. One, two points there, and then we're both in the same place at the same time." Nikki's eyes widened. "Oh, hold on, just wait a minute Colombo . . ."

"Colombo? You're not making sense, my friend."

Nikki waved a hand at him. "What if that Adonis dude is really a hired killer? He's not ugly and he's supposedly so in love with a woman old enough to be his mother."

"And loaded."

"No. I'm not loaded. I'm not. Three glasses does not make me loaded."

"No, Nik. Patrice. Money. *She's* loaded."

"Oh, totally. Totally loaded. Right. So maybe Patrice is paying off the brute to knock the people off who've wronged her."

"Where do you get this shit from?"

"I don't know. I'm brilliant." She laughed. "Right up there with Angela Lansbury, my friend."

"I'd say you watch too much TV," Jonah replied. "And sounds like old reruns. There are some decent new shows out in the world."

"No, I don't. I don't watch TV. I don't have time for television. I read."

"Sure. I'll check all of this out. Right now I have to go and pick up Petie from daycare and drop him with Alyssa, and then I have some questions to go ask."

"I'm gonna be real happy when you marry that girl."

"So will I, but we need to get you married first."

"We'll see."

"Sober up my friend, and go home." Jonah left and a waitress brought over a bottle of water and a basket of bread.

"Your friend said you wanted this."

"Thanks." Nikki ate a piece of the bread, downed the water, and then paid the bill and headed back to her room. She took a long bath and curled up in the hotel room's robe and, despite what she'd told Jonah, turned on the TV.

Why did it seem that every channel had a romance on it? She flipped the channels and still it seemed like love was in the air everywhere. She settled on the travel channel which, wouldn't you know, was running a segment on none other than destination weddings. She watched anyway. Number two was on the Greek isle of Mykonos, and Nikki had to admit that it did look beautiful. Maybe if she and Derek did go forward with their wedding plans that was where they should go. She chuckled to herself. Maybe it was fate? The gods of fate were directing the two of them to go to Greece and get married. Maybe, maybe, maybe . . . There were way too many maybes at the moment, and Nikki liked concrete. She didn't like that her brain was filled with wishy-washy theories and now her future was on that same wave length.

An ad came on the TV about weddings in Greece and the travel company to book it through. For the hell of it, Nikki took her laptop from her briefcase and then got online and looked up the travel company. The Web site's homepage showed Venus and Zeus in a wedding celebration. The images were beautiful. Each page had different gods on them and Nikki found herself amused at the synchronicity of it all. She shut off her laptop and decided to do as Jonah suggested and get some rest. She was getting a hammering headache.

A few hours later she woke up and felt quite a bit

better. It was already dark out, so she turned on the light and let her eyes adjust. She got up and headed to the bathroom. As she walked past the door she noticed a piece of paper on the floor. She picked it up and before she even unfolded it, she knew what it read: *Do you believe in fate?* Moros Apate Thanatos.

Thirty-nine

NO one likes being messed with, and Nikki was being messed with hard. Instead of being scared by the note, she found herself growing more and more pissed off. She got her stuff, checked out, and headed back home. Home. Even though she knew Derek had never really slept with Lily, the fact that he thought he had and he'd kept it from Nikki was still weighing on her.

Secrets. Yes, they'd both kept them, hadn't they? Sure, visiting Andrés was harmless because she'd done so in order to try to find out who was behind the shooting and Kenny's murder. But was it truly harmless? Was Andrés right when he'd said to her that she couldn't admit that she still had feelings for him?

She slammed her hands against the steering wheel. Damn it! If he hadn't come back home! She'd had plans. She and Derek wanted a family, and now all of this had snowballed and grown so huge and really bad. Being with Andrés had been simpler. Derek was far more complicated. Obviously. But she loved him. She adored him, so why was she still thinking about Andrés at all? Was it simply a question of what if . . . ? She let her mind take her there for a minute. What if she'd wound up with Andrés? Did she still love him? Honestly she didn't know if she'd ever loved him, not in the way she loved Derek. Andrés was easy and fun and passionate. The point being he was easy. He was one of those men that Nikki knew would always put her first, always be there for her, and would always be honest with her. That sounded good to her. The problem was that with Andrés she never felt challenged, and Derek put her to the test. The chemistry between Derek and her had always been potent. But would that chemistry eventually die and would she discover that love could be complicated by the fact that life took over, and would the lust that kept the chemistry going begin to dull? Time did that. It was well-known that keeping love alive was something that had to be worked at. Long-term marriages didn't get to those golden years without a little work. With Andrés, she didn't think that there would be a great deal of work, but would there ever be that combination of chemistry and love? It was there with Derek, but had their relationship taken such a sharp turn in the last week that they'd lost it?

She didn't know, but she had to find out. But before she addressed those deep questions inside her, she had to put this mystery together.

Someone knew she was at the Calistoga Ranch. Okay, take the easy ones first—Lily and Jonah. No way Jonah was the shooter. Lily was a definite possibility, but if she was behind this, she'd gotten sloppy by leaving that note. She could have easily told Jackson or anyone else back at Malveaux where she was. Simon didn't know where she was. He'd frantically texted her all day, and she'd replied telling him she needed some space and would be home later. So, he couldn't have known to let it slip in front of Patrice. There was also the possibility that someone had followed her from the ranch. It did look like Renee had to be taken off the list of suspects. She was in Hawaii, the self-serving, half-baked . . . Oh boy, did Nikki need to get over it.

She had to admit that although she was definitively that angry that someone had placed that note under the door in her hotel room, she was also extremely shaken. She would have liked to have had some time to figure this all out while enjoying the peace and quiet. She needed to put some things down in her notebook and work through some of these angles. She wondered if Jonah had gone by the winery and spoken to Derek's friends, and if so, what kind of stir it had caused. And she also couldn't help wondering if Lily had told Derek the truth yet.

Lots of questions.

Her phone rang and she recognized the number. One more question. Even though the timing wasn't convenient, it was definitely one she needed to answer.

Forty

"YOU said you needed to see me, so here I am." Nikki stood in Andrés' doorway, Isabel's puppy Camilla next to him.

"Come in, please. I'm still babysitting. Isabel decided to stay in the city with friends for a few days."

She followed him into the house. "So I see. She's so cute." He looked tired and worn. "Are you okay?" she asked.

He sat down on the couch in his family room, the light from his lamp casting shadows across his face. "No." He shook his head. The dog wiggled around Nikki.

"What is it?" she asked, worry straining her voice. She patted the puppy, who finally lay down next to her.

He looked at her. "It's you."

"We've been over this," she said.

"I know, and I can't shake it, and it's why I have to do what I have to do."

"I don't understand."

He sighed. "I don't know what I was thinking coming back here in the first place. I did have these ideas that you would see me and realize how good it had been between us. When I heard you were getting married, I thought I had to have one last try. One last chance. Like in the movies." He laughed, but his laughter was edged with sadness. "Stupid, isn't it? I thought I would be like the man in the fairy tale who comes and takes his true love from a man she doesn't really love. But I know now that you do really love Derek. I know my attempts were foolish, and I know now that I can never have you."

Nikki's stomach tightened.

"I'm going home tomorrow. For good. I cannot be near you or even in the same city. I need to go home and try to forget you. I have to. I've told the winery owners here that I won't be back. This is for good."

Nikki put her face in her hands. She wanted to tell him not to go. She really did. "I do love you, Andrés. I do. But I don't think it's in the way you want me to, and I wish it could be different because I know how much easier it would be with you."

He nodded and took her hands in his. "If, *if* things change . . . If your heart changes and you find in it that you are wrong, that there is the love for me, then you know where I will be. Because I know there is love between us, and I know that you may not feel it or see it, but if you ever do, I will be there for you. I *will*."

She kissed his cheek as a tear slid down his face. She walked out of his house for the last time, knowing she might have just passed up something she could never have again.

Forty-one

IT was after ten o'clock when Nikki unlocked the front door to Derek's place—their place. She didn't hear him or even see him at first as Ollie bounded toward her, tail wagging. She bent down and he gave her a sloppy kiss. "I missed you, too."

That's when she heard a deep sob from the other room.

"Derek?"

He didn't answer. She walked into the living room where she found Derek in his leather chair, his face in his hands, a brandy snifter on the table next to him.

"Derek?"

He looked up, his eyes bloodshot, swollen. "We have to fix this," he said.

She came to him. "What is it? What's going on?"

He just shook his head. "So much. We have to fix this, Nik."

"I know. We will, but you have to tell me why you are so upset. You knew I'd come home, right?"

"No. I didn't know and now everything is worse."

"What is worse? What are you talking about?"

"Tristan. He tried to kill Savannah tonight. He's the one. He's the one who did all of this. He tried to kill you. He killed Kenny. And now his own wife. She's in surgery right now. I found her, Nik. I found her behind the wine bar in a pool of blood, and when I looked up, there was Tristan all bloodied. He had a knife in his hand. He dropped it. He says he didn't do it. He says he found her and then tried to use the bar phone to call 911, and then he saw the knife by her and picked it up. But come on," he sobbed, "that's crazy. He did this, and he's caused all of this between you and me, and I am so sorry, baby. I am so, so sorry. Please tell me that we can fix this, because I can't, I don't want to live without you. I've seen way too much in the last few days, learned way too much about people I thought I knew, and you know what I realize?"

She shook her head.

"I realized you're the only one I really know. You're the only who knows me. Through all of this insanity, I knew you would keep me grounded and I prayed I would keep you grounded. But I let you down. And I am so sorry."

She wrapped her arms around him and held tight. "We can and we will fix this."

Forty-two

TRISTAN was in jail and his wife was fighting for her life. Nikki and Derek woke up the next morning in each other's arms, both committed to trying to make things right between them.

Lily had told Derek everything the day before, and he couldn't believe it. Jonah had let everyone else at the hotel know that they could go home. Nikki wanted to go and see Savannah in the hospital.

Savannah was in the ICU and Nikki had to do some fast talking to get past the gestapo of nurses, but she was able to make it happen. When she saw Savannah she couldn't believe it was the same woman she'd come to know over the last few days. Savannah looked even tinier under the bed sheets than she normally did. Her face was drawn and pale. Her lips tight, eyes closed. She hadn't woken from her surgery. She was full of tubes and IVs. It frightened Nikki to think that Tristan had done this to her. It frightened her to think anyone was capable of this.

Nikki came to her side. "I'm so sorry this happened to you. I'm sorry that I wasn't a better hostess and that I was rude to you. No one deserves this. Tristan will go away for a long time. He'll never be able to hurt you again."

Savannah opened her eyes slowly and she focused on Nikki.

"Hang on, hang on I'll get a nurse."

"No," Savannah whispered. "Tristan . . ."

"He's in jail. You're safe."

Savannah shook her head. "No. Please. Nancy. Find out . . ." One of the monitors rang out and the next thing Nikki knew she was being pushed aside as the room filled with personnel.

"She's crashing!" a nurse yelled. "Get me a crash cart!"

"Code blue, room two eleven," rang out over the hospital intercom system.

Nikki stood back and felt like she was in a dream. Was Savannah going to die? She said a silent prayer that the poor woman would live. She thought about Tristan and Savannah's children. Here their mother might die and their father was a killer. Or was he? Why was Savannah saying "no" when Nikki mentioned Tristan's name? Was it just that she was in shock? And Nancy? Why was she talking about Nancy? Zach's ex-wife? Or was she just confusing Nikki with Nancy? People said strange things under duress.

As Nikki watched the doctors and nurses work on Savannah, she kept praying that Savannah would survive this ordeal.

Nikki heard the sound of Savannah's heart monitor begin beeping again. She looked up.

"She's back," one of the doctors said and continued on with more orders.

A nurse breezed by as Nikki remained in the doorway. Nikki grabbed her arm. "Is she going to be okay?"

"Who are you?" the nurse asked.

"A friend."

"She's alive still. That's pretty much all I can say."

"Thank you." Nikki left the hospital, head down, hands shoved into her jean pockets. She sat in her car for several minutes, stunned.

Nancy? Nancy? What had Nikki learned about Zach's absent wife? Simon said she was crazy—or at least obsessive. Savannah claimed the divorce was ugly. She was an artist. No children because she couldn't conceive. Obsessive people went right along with controlling. What about the identity theory that Alyssa had helped Nikki with? And supposedly Nancy was in Puerto Vallarta. But what if she wasn't in Mexico? What if she murdered Kenny, shot at Nikki, and tried to kill Savannah? But why?

Nikki didn't know why. Savannah was a friend of Nancy's—or supposedly was. What was the common thread in all of this? Derek.

Moros Apate Thanatos. The killer's signature. Moros meant impending doom. Apate was the goddess of deceit. Thanatos was death. Doom, deceit, death. Someone in this clan was warning Nikki of impending doom, letting her know they were not who they said they were, and ultimately causing death.

Nikki had an idea. It was a long shot and out there,

but she didn't have much to go on. There was an angle
here. This whole Greek god thing meant something to
this killer. Her gut told her that the killer wasn't smart in
the way she thought maybe Jackson or Lily had been—
and she hadn't discounted them yet. But this person was
psychotic or had lost the marbles rattling around in the
brain.

Nikki headed back to the winery to check her theory,
because she didn't want Savannah to possibly die thinking her husband was behind bars for something he didn't
do. Nikki was convinced that Jonah had the wrong man
in jail.

Forty-three

NIKKI pulled up in front of the Malveaux Hotel and Spa and spotted Jackson and Lily putting their bags in their rental car. Zach was rolling his luggage out the front archway as well.

Nikki got out of her Camry and walked over. "You're all leaving?" she asked.

"Yeah. Sorry, Nikki, the police told us we were free to go home, and we have to get back to our kids and our lives. I'm so sorry this has happened." Jackson gave her a hug.

Lily took her hands. "And I'm sorry for any grief that I caused you and Derek. I know this is all going to work out for you."

"We're just all a little shell-shocked," Zach said. "I'm actually picking Nancy up at the airport and she's going to drive home to L.A. with me. We've been talking and with all of this that's happened, I think we're going to try to work this out."

"Nancy?" Nikki asked.

"Yes," Zach replied. "She is my wife."

"And she's in Mexico? In Puerto Vallarta?"

"Yes. Or she was. She's on a plane right now. Her flight is due in at two thirty this afternoon, so I need to get on the road. We've talked about this. Maybe you don't remember because of everything that's gone on this week."

"No. I'm sorry. I remember. It's just, well, Savannah mentioned her name in the hospital and . . ." She waved a hand in the air. "It's nothing."

"Savannah and Nance are friends. Maybe that's why."

"You were at the hospital?" Jackson asked. "And Savannah was talking?"

"I was just there. It wasn't good. She went into cardiac arrest but she's hanging on."

Lily brought a hand to her mouth. "Oh, my gosh. Poor thing. This is unbelievable."

"Yes," Nikki replied.

Lily hugged her. "Again, Nikki, please forgive me. I really am sorry."

Nikki nodded. "Thank you. Have a safe trip home."

"We will." Jackson hugged her, too, and then Zach.

They all got into their cars. Nikki watched as they drove off, wondering if a killer hadn't just gotten away.

She walked through the archways of the hotel and looked for Derek. She spotted Marco. "Ah, *bellisima*, what a terrible, terrible week this has been. No?"

"You could say that."

"I have good news though."

"Really? I could use some good news right about now."

"Patrice and Adonis are leaving today." He clapped his hands together. "For good." He smiled widely.

"Seriously? What brought that on?"

"A lot, a lot of money. She settled with Derek and Simon for a lot more than she deserved."

"She certainly doesn't deserve anything."

"I agree," Marco said, "but at least she will be bye-bye, arrivederci. And Simon and Violet and me can go forward with our lives."

"That is good, great in fact," she said.

"And you and Derek, too."

Nikki nodded.

"Uh-oh, bellisima, why so sad? Why so gloomy? What is it the matter?"

"It's me and Derek, I don't know. There's been so much that has happened in the last few days and with things that I've learned . . . I don't know if this will work for us."

Marco came around from behind the counter and took her hands in his. "Bellisima, you speak nonsense. Look what Simon and I have endured over the last few years from cheating, lying, his monster mother, and then some. But we decided that our love was stronger than all of that. We made it through the worst things possible, and now our love holds and I am telling you that this will be forever. If it was easy, then it would not be worth it. The good times would be, hmmm . . . they would be flat. Nothing interesting. Nothing to grow from. Nothing to appreciate. It is out of the hard times that we learn to love more, be thankful for more. It is this time that you will look back on and know that it was what your love needed to make it even better." He kissed her on each cheek.

She kissed him back. "You know, you are a wise man."

He shrugged. "Maybe. And you are a wise woman, so follow your heart."

"I will. By the way, have you seen Derek around?"

"Oh, yes, he did say to tell you that he took Ollie to the vet. He ate something we think that made him sick."

"What? Oh no! Is he okay?"

"I think so. Derek wanted to be sure because he wouldn't eat and he was vomiting. Maybe a flu."

"No. Dogs don't get flu bugs. I don't think. That doesn't sound good." Nikki took her cell from her purse and dialed Derek's number. It went straight to voicemail. "Damn. If you hear from him, have him call me. I'm going down to the house."

"I will do that. No worries, bellisima. Ollie will be good, and you and Derek will be good."

She smiled at him, hoping and praying he was right. She couldn't imagine losing Ollie. Not on top of everything else. She loved that dog. She called the vet's office, and they told her that Derek and the vet were in with Ollie at the moment. She thought about going down there and asked, but they told her they would call her back if they thought it was necessary. For now it looked as if Ollie was going to be okay.

"Do you know what's wrong?" Nikki asked.

The receptionist asked to put her on hold. Nikki got into her car and headed down the hill to the house, waiting for the girl to come back on the line. When she did, she said, "It would appear that he got into some type of rat poison."

"Rat poison? We don't keep rat poison around."

"The good news is that he will be okay. Dr. Green called poison control and we've done everything here by the book. We're just going to monitor him for another hour or so. But Dr. Green says he'll be just fine."

Nikki took a deep breath. "Okay. Thank you." She hung up the phone and parked in front of the house. Rat poison. Where had Ollie gotten into that?

Then it struck her: maybe he didn't get into it. Maybe someone had fed it to him. And as she went inside the house to her office, a text from an unknown caller came across her phone. *Moros Apate Thanatos.*

Forty-four

NIKKI made sure all the doors and windows were locked. She thought about calling Simon to come down, but then she realized how silly she was being. No one was in the house, and no was getting in the house.

She went into the kitchen and took out a bag of solace—potato chips. It was her one junk food habit and when anxiety hit, the salty, crispy treats were a necessity. She grabbed a bottle of water from the fridge and went into the office to see if her "shot in the dark" was even remotely correct.

Nancy was a link. Why Nancy would want anyone dead Nikki still didn't know. Nancy was an artist. A lot of artists had Web sites. She got online and typed in Nancy with her married name. Nothing. Nikki went into the family room where the college annual they'd all looked at the other night and the photo album that Savannah had left still were.

Nancy's maiden name had been Flowers. Okay, Nancy Flowers. Nikki went back to the Internet and Googled Nancy Flowers. Sure enough she got a hit. There was a realtor, an Amnesty International gal with the same name, and then tons of Nancy's Flowers for florist shops. On the second page she found what she was looking for, and hit the link.

Nancy was quite a talented artist. Nikki studied the photo of her. A little bit of an older version of the woman in the college photos, but still very pretty. She didn't *look* crazy. The bio photo was of her seated on a rock, overlooking an azure sea. The caption beneath it read, "Santorini, Greece." Nikki's stomach sank. She then hit the portfolio page. There were landscape paintings of what looked to be Italy, the London Bridge, and the Eiffel Tower. There were paintings Nancy had done of a Spanish woman playing a violin. She had a group of these, and then what looked to be cultural pieces of parts of Mexico. She appeared to like various cultures and settings. The second page, though, was what got Nikki, and proved to her that she was onto something. That page was filled with mythological creatures, gods, and goddesses. Nikki then went to Nancy's client page. She scrolled through a list of clients, noting that Nancy had done quite a bit of commercial work on print ads. And that's where she found what she needed.

Nikki leaned back as she pressed the link to Kincaid Advertising and Publicity Firm. Zach's last name was Kincaid.

The link was no longer live. Nikki then went back to Nancy's site and searched through it. She found a group of ads that Nancy had worked on for Kincaid. Nikki caught her breath. There was the ad she'd seen online the day before while licking her wounds at the Calistoga Ranch—Venus and Zeus getting married. It was for the travel agency.

Nancy was not the criminal. But Nikki knew who was.

Nikki then proceeded to try to find all airlines that flew from Oakland to Puerto Vallarta and vice versa. This took her some time, but she was pretty sure she'd acquired a complete list. After that she began checking flight times for that day. There was no flight from any airline landing in Oakland from Puerto Vallarta.

"Zach lied," she said out loud.

The hair on the back of her neck stood on end as she knew there was another presence in the room. Before she could turn around or get out of her chair, a knife was pressed to her throat, and Zach whispered in her ear, "Do you believe in fate?"

Forty-five

ZACH had Nikki tied up, and as he started to cut masking tape to presumably place across her mouth, she asked him again, "Why?"

He closed his eyes briefly and shook his head. When he opened his eyes, Nikki could see she was looking at someone who had truly lost it.

"Why? I guess since I'm going to put down my impending doom on you, I owe you an explanation." He laughed. "Funny thing is, Nikki, I was going to leave you alone. Initially I'd planned to kill you. I'm apparently not as great a shot as I thought. I used to be better when I hunted all the time, but marriage sucks the life out of you. I had to stop hunting," he whined, mocking a woman's voice. "I had to work harder. I had to do this and that and pay more attention to her." He shook his head. "Please. When does a man ever get to be a man? That bitch would never let me just be a man. Always busting my balls. And I tried. Believe me, I tried hard to please her. I lost my job, and so I started my own agency. I put our savings into it. Then the bitch left me. She just left me. Blamed me for everything. Blamed me for not getting her pregnant. Blamed me for not being like Kenny, or Derek, or Tristan, or even Jackson. For not being the success that all those guys we went to school with had become. You know I even tried to get Kenny to work with me? I had ads for that stupid magazine of his and he wouldn't cut me any kind of slack. No deal. And Derek? I tried to get him as a client, but apparently he said all of your marketing is in-house. Something you're in charge of. I lost my business on top of everything else. I lost everything that I knew and believed about myself."

"So you murdered Kenny for not cutting you any slack? And you wanted to kill me because our ads are done in-house? Zach, that doesn't make a lot of sense. Think about it." Jeez, who was she kidding here? This guy was a murderer. His theories behind why he killed didn't have to make sense to anyone but himself. Bottom line, the guy was twisted and sick in the head. Nikki knew she should be more frightened at that moment, and she was pretty scared, however she also knew that if she could keep him talking, keep him distracted, that maybe she could get out of this.

"Kenny, yes, and also for being such a blowhard jerk for all of these years, and for screwing Savannah, because everyone knew that was going on. I was trying to help Tristan out. I kinda like the guy. His own fault for picking up the knife. Idiot. She's the one who put the word divorce in my wife's ear."

"And me? Why me?"

He laughed. "Because why should Derek Malveaux always win in the end? The golden boy, the rich kid, the one who has it all? Always had it all. And Nancy made such a big deal of it to me. It was always *Derek this,* and *Derek that.* You know one day she even remarked that she wished she'd had a chance at Derek and married him." He shook his head. "I'm sick and tired of everyone always coming out on top but me. Kenny had his booming company. Derek has money and you and all this happiness. It's wrong! When is it my turn? Me? I'm a good guy. I am! You know when the invitation came for the wedding, and Nancy started in about how great Derek is, how perfect he was, blah, blah, goddamn blah . . . I figured I'm over it. Not everyone else besides me gets to win all the time."

"You're really disturbed."

"Maybe."

"And Nancy?"

"Dead. I took her on a little deep-sea fishing expedition. Bye-bye." He wiggled his fingers.

"You're never going to get away with this."

"I will. And then I'm going to disappear."

"Let me guess. Greece?"

"I'm not telling." He winked at her.

Goosebumps traveled down Nikki's arms and her stomach sank. Keep him talking. "What's the Greek angle? Just a scare thing?"

"Nah. That's all Nancy. She loved that mythology crap and used to blab on about it. I kind of liked the idea of gods of fate at work. The nasty ones anyway. It's made this game far more interesting for me. Anyway, you've had enough chitchat time. That's the problem with all of you women. You talk too much!" He placed the tape over her mouth as she futilely tried to shove him away with her bound legs, only managing to get in one good kick. "That hurt, you bitch." He slapped her hard across her face.

This wasn't going well. Then Nikki heard the front door open and Derek's voice call her name.

Zach got behind her and placed the knife at her neck. "Oh, perfect," he whispered.

"Nikki?"

Nikki's eyes widened as she spotted Derek come around the corner and into the office. He stopped and stared. She knew it was taking him a few seconds to register what he was seeing. "Zach, what are you doing?"

"Come on, buddy. Don't you believe in fate?"

Where was Ollie? If he knew she was in trouble, he'd be right there. Nikki closed her eyes tight. If the son of a bitch had killed her dog . . .

"Let her go, man. I don't know what this is about, but let her go and we can talk about it."

"Nah. Nothing to talk about." He sighed and moved to the side, still keeping the knife on her throat. She could feel him reaching into his pocket and wondered what he was trying to get. Then she saw what he was after and knew they were both in grave danger. As Zach brought the gun up to shoot Derek, he said, "Two birds. Moros Apate Thanatos, my friend."

It all happened fast—Derek dove to the side as the gunshot rang out. Nikki felt the pressure of the knife against her neck and a trickle of blood. She grew dizzy and began to lose consciousness. As her vision faded and Zach stood, she saw Ollie in the doorway, either he was weaving or it was her fading that made him look like that. *Poor Ollie*, she thought drowsily. *I hope my pal is all right.*

As everything went dark, she heard the commotion. Derek was yelling, Ollie was growling and barking, there was screaming, and then another gunshot rang out.

Forty-six

WHEN Nikki woke, she didn't recognize where she was at first. But then the sounds surrounding her clued her in. Blips, bleeps and dings. The hospital. The smell of antiseptic was unmistakable. Her throat burned miserably. It took a minute for her eyes to adjust and when they finally did, she spotted Simon in a chair dozing. She said his name, and then realized she couldn't say it too loudly. But it was enough to snap him to.

He rushed to her side. "Oh my God, Tink. I thought, I thought . . . Oh, we all thought . . ." Tears streamed down his face.

"Thought what?"

"I thought we might have lost you. And I couldn't have gone on without you. My God, who would I have gone to Barneys with? And who would I drink copious amounts of champagne with, and make fun of each other with? And who in the hell could I call Goldilocks, Snow

White, and Tinker Bell? No one. Only you! Only you, and you're alive."

"What happened?" she uttered.

"That bad man, he tried to kill you, but thank God for Ollie and your knight in shining armor, my darling brother. Ollie attacked Zach, and Derek shot him and he's dead. But he hurt you, honey."

"How bad? Where's Derek?"

Simon put a finger on her throat. "He cut about an inch and you lost some blood. But you're alive, you're here!"

"Of course she is." Derek walked in and took her hand. "Is he scaring you?"

Nikki nodded. "A little."

"He's pulling the drama queen act."

Simon rolled his eyes. "Maybe a little, but I wanted her to know how much I love her. How much we love her."

"I know," she whispered. "I do know."

"Good. I'm going to find Marco and Violet. Marco took her to the cafeteria. He'll be delighted to know you're awake." He leaned over her and kissed her cheek. "I do love you, Tink. And if you ever play detective again, I'm never going to go shopping with you. And forget the champagne. And, well, I'll just start calling you Nikki. No more fancy schmancy nicknames, sister. You can bet on it."

"Now that would be a crime," Nikki said.

"It would." He turned around and marched out of the room.

Derek's grasp on her hand tightened. He shook his head. "I just came from talking to the doctor, and your throat will be sore for some time, but you're going to be fine."

She smiled. "What about Savannah? Tristan?"

He sighed. "Tristan has been released from jail. He's with Savannah now. She's still critical but they think she's going to make it."

"Thank goodness."

"And Zach is . . . ?"

"Dead. Ollie is a miracle. When I brought him back from the vet he was woozy, because they had to pump his stomach and they gave him some pain medication. But as soon as he realized we were in trouble, that you were in trouble, he sobered up real quick. Leapt about ten feet and took Zach down. It was just long enough for me to grab the gun, and when I saw that he was going for you again to . . . to . . ." He wiped tears from his face. "To finish what he started, I shot him. I had to."

"You saved me," Nikki said.

"I love you so much, Nik. And now I just want us to get past all of this and move on. I paid Patrice a lot of money. She finally agreed to go."

"I know. Simon told me."

"Of course." He laughed. "My brother and his big mouth. I wanted to be the one to tell you."

"He means well."

"He does." Derek brought her hand to his lips and kissed it. "Listen to me for a minute. I have to tell you this, and I know that you're not in any sort of state to make any decisions right now, but you need to know exactly how I feel."

"Okay."

"I love you, Nikki, and after all we've been through,

I love you even more. You make my life worth living. I couldn't have gone on without you. I really don't think that I could have. I don't ever want to lose you. Not ever. I'll do anything to win your confidence in me again. I'll never keep secrets from you. I'll always be honest. I'll love you when things are crappy and when they're fantastic. I'll be your best friend and your lover. All I know is that I want to commit myself to you forever, and we don't need a big fancy wedding. We don't need four hundred guests. We just need each other."

She looked at him and her eyes filled with tears.

"So if you'll still have me, I need you to start thinking."

"Thinking about . . . ?" She smiled.

"Where we're getting married and who to invite. The fewer people the better."

"I agree."

He laughed. "That sounds to me like you'll still have me."

"I love you, Derek. Of course I'll still have you. We are getting married," Nikki said. She believed it. Ninety-five percent of her believed it, anyway, but that was good enough for now. However, she knew that there was a man who still loved her back in Spain, and there was a part of her that would always love him more than she'd ever been willing to admit to herself. Maybe someday their paths would cross again.

Epilogue

Eight months later

THE bride and groom stood on top of the hillside, cresting the famous wine valley region below. She wore a simple ivory strapless sheath and was barefoot with a single pink hibiscus flower in her hair above her ear.

There were only a handful of family and close friends. They'd written their own vows. Heartfelt and beautiful. Meaningful. For those who never believed the day would ever come, they had shown them. Many had never expected this wedding to take place. Ever. Hearts had been broken along the way, lives had been changed, but their love had blossomed and held them through it all.

And as the pastor pronounced them man and wife, Nikki Sands (now Nikki Malveaux) stood on her tiptoes and kissed her groom, knowing she'd just married her soul mate.

RECIPE INDEX